For Reasons that Remain Unclear

Mart Crowley

A SAMUEL FRENCH ACTING EDITION

SAMUEL FRENCH

FOUNDED 1830

SAMUELFRENCH.COM
SAMUELFRENCH-LONDON.CO.UK

FOR PRODUCTION ENQUIRIES

UNITED STATES AND CANADA
Info@SamuelFrench.com
1-866-598-8449

UNITED KINGDOM AND EUROPE
Theatre@SamuelFrench-London.co.uk
020-7255-4302

Each title is subject to availability from Samuel French, depending upon country of performance. Please be aware that *For Reasons that Remain Unclear* may not be licensed by Samuel French in your territory. Professional and amateur producers should contact the nearest Samuel French office or licensing partner to verify availability.

MUSIC USE NOTE

Licensees are solely responsible for obtaining formal written permission from copyright owners to use copyrighted music in the performance of this play and are strongly cautioned to do so. If no such permission is obtained by the licensee, then the licensee must use only original music that the licensee owns and controls. Licensees are solely responsible and liable for all music clearances and shall indemnify the copyright owners of the play(s) and their licensing agent, Samuel French, against any costs, expenses, losses and liabilities arising from the use of music by licensees. Please contact the appropriate music licensing authority in your territory for the rights to any incidental music.

IMPORTANT BILLING AND CREDIT REQUIREMENTS

If you have obtained performance rights to this title, please refer to your licensing agreement for important billing and credit requirements.

FOR REASONS THAT REMAIN UNCLEAR was first presented on November 9, 1993, at the Olney Theatre in Olney, Maryland., James A. Peosta and Bill Graham Jr., producing directors. The scenery was designed by James Wolk, the lighting was by Howard Werner, and the play was directed by John Going.

The cast was:

PATRICK	Philip Anglim
CONRAD	Ken Ruta
WAITER	Fred Iocova

For Millie and Toby Rowland

On the occasion of their fiftieth wedding anniversary—

Without whose instigation, encouragement and love ...

The stage is dark and uninhabited. Through a floor-length window center right, the intense violet light of a dying summer day— poised between late afternoon and early evening—slowly fades up to "half" to partially reveal a light wood-paneled bed/sitting room in the Hassler Hotel in Rome.

Brocade portieres with sheer center curtains cover the tall glass doors which open onto a shallow balcony overlooking the Piazza Di Spagna. The exterior shutters are folded back, admitting the refracted iridescence. The glass doors are slightly open, and a gentle breeze stirs the gauzy fabric, casting soft patterns across the heavily shadowed interior.

Upstage left on a wide raised platform, there is a double bed with its covers and linen sheets neatly turned down. The headboard and dust ruffle are of the same brocade as the draperies. On either side of the bed there are built-in night tables above which there are brass "extension" wall lamps in mirrored panels, presently not illuminated. On the stage-right table there is a bottle of mineral water and a tumbler on a tray. On the stage-left table there is a panel of service buttons.

Along the left wall is a chest of drawers with a Venetian-style mirror above it. On top of the chest, there is a handsome toiletry case and various smart toilet articles in evidence—cologne, talcum, a comb and brush. A door center left leads to a marble-walled bath. Luxurious towels, featuring the name and logo of the hotel, can be seen folded over a brass warming rack.

Downstage of the bathroom door, against the wall there is a luggage stand with an expensive suitcase on it. Out from the wall, almost at the curtain line, there is a low drum-like upholstered dressing stool.

Within wood-paneled arches, supported by slender marble columns,

*in the up-center-right and stage-right walls of the sitting area,
there are unlit Venetian-style glass sconces with half shades.
Standing away from the wall, there is a brocade settee facing
front, a brocade lounge chair angled stage right of it, and a low
drinks/coffee table before them.*

*All wooden pieces of furniture are reproductions of traditional Italian
designs of the eighteenth century. The upholstered ones are of the
fascist period.*

*A man's pale gray linen suit on a Hassler clothes hanger is neatly
folded over the back of a chair. In a flat wicker basket on the seat
of the settee there are some stacks of colorful shirts and some
white silk boxer-style undershorts which have been returned from
the hotel laundry. The basket is covered with a piece of paper on
top of which sits a pair of freshly shined Italian loafers.*

*The door to the public corridor is upstage center. After a moment, it is
unlocked from the outside. It is a bolt of the European variety,
which requires several revolutions of the key. Presently, two male
figures enter, silhouetted to the audience by the light spill from
the hallway. Even in the chiaroscuro, it is apparent that the
FIRST MAN is in dark apparel, the SECOND in light-colored
clothing and that both are wearing sunglasses The SECOND is
laden with shopping bags from smart stores on the Via Condotti.*

*It is just after six p.m., and a nearby church bell is ringing the
Angelus.)*

FIRST MAN. *(Crossing to balcony, with enthusiasm.)* Dio mio,
as they say, just look at that view! Oh, I was hoping your room would
be on the front of the hotel and have a view of the steps and piazza!
*(He parts the sheers, widens the doors and scans the view. A long
shaft of cool purplish light bisects the room. Street sounds rush in.
The SECOND MAN closes the entry and goes through the shadows to
deposit the shopping bags on the bed.)* Magnificent! Is that the dome
of St. Peter's in the distance? What am I saying? Of course it is!
(Pointing.) I'm staying just to the right of it. My God, that's a

heavenly sight!

(The SECOND MAN stands silently observing the FIRST MAN for a moment before snapping on the lamp on the night table, introducing a small pool of warm, rosy light to the area surrounding him. In spite of his dark glasses, he is revealed to be in his early forties, trim and average-looking, but well-groomed in a creased ecru linen suit and soft white shirt without a tie.)

SECOND MAN. Yes. And magic hour, to boot. Very picture-postcard, don't you think?

(The FIRST MAN, at the balcony window observing the view through his sunglasses, turns inside to reveal that he is in his late fifties, dressed in the black garb and Roman collar of a priest.)

FIRST MAN. Oh, if only I could stamp and mail this moment! *(Turns back to react to bells tolling.)* And just listen, Patrick ... the Angelus, so *near* you can almost touch it!
PATRICK *(SECOND MAN)*. Mmm. Almost, but not quite.
FIRST MAN. Is it coming from Trinità dei Monti next door?
PATRICK. Too far away for that, Father.
FIRST MAN. *(Faces PATRICK again.)* Now, please, do call me Conrad. Father sounds so ....
PATRICK. Paternal?
CONRAD *(FIRST MAN). Respectful!*
PATRICK. *(Putting room key in side jacket pocket.)* You must take off your sunglasses so you can really get the full-tilt "schmear."
CONRAD. *(Re: sunglasses.)* Ohh! Had them on so long I completely forgot! Wear them all the time in California. I really don't like the sun much.
PATRICK. Well, then, you live in the wrong place if you don't like to be sun-kissed.
CONRAD. Maybe it's something I inherited from my mother.

She never liked the sun. Said she couldn't see for the light! *(Picking up from before.)* The full-tilt *what*?

PATRICK. Schmear. The whole deal.

CONRAD. Oh. That's not Italian, is it?

PATRICK. Yiddish.

CONRAD. Oh. *(Removes his glasses, turns back to luxuriate in the view.)* Oh, oh, oh, oh, *ohhhhh*! Well, yes, that does make a difference! Now I can really see what's going on!

(Turns back to PATRICK, who now slowly takes off his glasses.)

PATRICK. And now we can see each other too. *(Dryly.)* And not through rose-colored glasses.

CONRAD. *(Laughs.)* Yes, finally! I couldn't make out your eyes behind your shades at lunch. From here they look blue. Very, very blue.

PATRICK. They're green. It's the light playing tricks. *(Looks away.)* And *your* eyes are ....

CONRAD. Bloodshot, probably, after all that wonderful wine!

PATRICK. *(Staring off.)* Brown. Dark, dark brown.

CONRAD. It's the black Irish in me. I must say, you have better sight than I do. *(Re: bells.)* Ahh, just listen to that! Such a clean sound. *(Turns out, listens; after a moment.)* Where do you think it's coming from, San Silvestro? Or one of the churches in the Piazza del Popolo?

PATRICK. Who knows? In this town church bells ring like telephones.

(PATRICK moves around to the other side of the bed as CONRAD steps back into the room. PATRICK begins to empty the shopping bags and put the contents away: Armani trousers, Gucci agenda boxes, brand-name cologne bags, and a Cartier watchcase.)

CONRAD. Such a treat, isn't it? Coming from Los Angeles,

where you never hear church bells at all!

PATRICK. *(Aside.)* Mmm. The lost Angelus of Los Angeles.

CONRAD. *(Chuckles.)* Isn't that odd?

PATRICK. *(Wryly.)* One more odd thing.

CONRAD. You mean about L.A.? Or our both *being* from L.A.?

PATRICK. That too.

CONRAD. Absolutely incredible! Imagine, meeting each other halfway round the world! *(Turns to the open window, listens.)* Such a reassuring sound! We're really cheated in L.A. It's so spread-out, we can't even experience one of the most reassuring things in the world.

PATRICK. For me, one of the most reassuring things in the world is a plate of pasta.

CONRAD. *(Hesitates, then laughs.)* Well, then, you're in the *right* place!

PATRICK. And so are you if it's ding-donging that you find reassuring.

(CONRAD becomes aware that PATRICK is staring at him, turns toward him as they both listen to the bells for a moment.)

CONRAD. There's that faraway look of yours again. What are you thinking, if I may ask? You seem lost.

PATRICK *(Focusing.)* Forgive me. *(After a moment, agreeably.)* I must admit, I too love to hear the bells tolling. But for some reason the sound always makes me sad.

CONRAD. Sad?

PATRICK. It's a melancholy sound. But, at least, a bell is something civilized man has made when he's made so many terrible things.

CONRAD. The call of angels.

PATRICK. A bell is an elegant ... noble creation—as admirable as the quaint little rituals man's invented for ringing his brainchild.

CONRAD. *(Amused.)* You mean a "quaint little ritual" like the Angelus.

PATRICK. That too. The Angelus, the time of day, New Year's.

All ring-out-the news occasions are all the same to me, no matter what. And no matter how joyous—even if it were the end of a war—I don't know, it's a plaintive sound.

CONRAD. Funny. I think just the opposite. Even a bell tolling at a funeral is a joyous sound to me. I remember that, when my mother died, thinking that she was so much better off.

PATRICK. Well, I do find a death knell joyous! You think it's just the beginning of something. I think it's joyous because it's the end. *Finally*! Over! Hallelujah! I *hope*!

CONRAD. Now, don't tell me you don't believe in the hereafter.

PATRICK. Let's just say, I believe in the *future*.

CONRAD. And when we die?

PATRICK. I can't conceive of what might be in store, but I hope that when this is over, *that's* it. I don't want any more. Bad or good. And how good can it get? I can't think of anything more maddening than an eternal orgasm.

(CONRAD chuckles a bit self-consciously. PATRICK snaps on the left bedside lamp, widening the warm circle of light.)

CONRAD. Nice little room you have here!

PATRICK. It's majestic. But I call it home. *(The Angelus ceases as PATRICK comes around the bed and crosses to the panel in the upstage wall, right of the corridor door. Indicates.)* Please ... sit anywhere you like.

CONRAD. Thank you.

PATRICK. *(Re: suit and basket on the settee.)* That is, anywhere you can find a seat. Here, let me get the laundry out of the way.

CONRAD. It must cost a fortune to stay here.

(CONRAD crosses from the window toward the settee.)

PATRICK. Well, I'm not paying for it, the brothers Warner are. And, yes, ... it costs a *fortune* to stay here. *(CONRAD laughs as*

PATRICK snaps on a wall switch, illuminating the sconces, which infuse the stage right sitting area with the same rosy glow as stage left. Crossing down behind settee:) Sorry things are messy.

(CONRAD has reached the chair first, picks up the hanger with the pale linen suit.)

CONRAD. Such beautiful clothes.
PATRICK. As you've probably heard—they make the man.

(PATRICK leans over the settee to pick up the wicker basket of laundry with the shoes on top and takes the hanger from CONRAD.)

CONRAD. Such beautiful shoes.
PATRICK. If the shoe fits, charge it!

(PATRICK goes to the bed, puts down the wicker basket, picks up the shoes and takes them to the upholstered dressing stool, drops them on top of it and takes the suit of clothes into the bathroom.)

CONRAD. *(During the above.)* You should see my room! Like the inside of a crashed plane! Compared to me, you're the very soul of immaculacy.
PATRICK. *(Offstage.)* "The soul of immaculacy!" That sounds so Catholic—when all I am is anal-compulsive. Anyway, it's all show. Inside, I'm well ….
CONRAD. What?
PATRICK. *(Offstage.)* Like the inside of a crashed plane. You say you're staying on the right side of St. Peter?

(CONRAD settles on the left arm of the settee.)
CONRAD. Well, I always try to stay on the right side.

(Chuckles.) A big old palazzo which is a convent now. The nuns are away for the summer. Of course, my room is nothing grand like this.

(PATRICK reenters, goes to pick up the pair of loafers on top of the dressing stool, and sits down on it. He starts to take off his shoes and put on the loafers.)

PATRICK. The first time I came to Rome I stayed in a place laughingly called the Grande Hotel—not the famous, fancy one near the Piazza della Repùblica—a little dump in Trastevere. It was so awful, in fact, that I stumbled home pissed-out-of-my-mind one night, took a Magic Marker and, in front of the name, I printed the words "Not Very." The *padrona* wasn't at all thrilled I'd rechristened his establishment the "Not Very Grande Hotel." *(CONRAD laughs. PATRICK finishes changing shoes. Re: loafers.)* Ouu, does that feel better! My mother always used to say there's nothing that relaxes you like changing your shoes. Would you like a pair of slippers? I just charged some very smart velour ones the other day. We look to be about the same size.
CONRAD. *(Hesitantly.)* Oh, no, I don't think ....
PATRICK. *(Gets up.)* Please. Get comfortable and stay awhile.
CONRAD. *(Relenting.)* Well, I have been on my feet since dawn. You walk much more in Rome than in New York even. And, of course, in L.A. you never walk anywhere at all. *(PATRICK exits into the bath, taking his original pair of shoes with him as CONRAD crosses to the dressing stool.)* ... If you've been here three months and the movie studio is paying for it, why haven't you rented a place?

(PATRICK returns with a pair of black velour slippers. CONRAD starts to take the slippers from PATRICK, but PATRICK puts his hand on CONRAD's shoulder and gently pushes him down on the stool, then kneels before him and begins to unlace his shoes.)
PATRICK. *(During the above.)* I'm a hotel boy. Love hotels.

Lived in the Algonquin for four years.

CONRAD. The Algonquin? Oh, yes. The place with the famous table.

(PATRICK removes CONRAD's shoes and puts the slippers on his feet.)

PATRICK. Checked in one night when a play of mine was in rehearsal. The play closed, but I stayed on. And on and on. Till the money ran out. To me, being in a hotel is like being in a wonderful hospital where all the doctors and nurses are dressed up in disguise as waiters and maids. Room service is my idea of therapy!

CONRAD. *(Re: PATRICK's action.)* You make a pretty good valet!

PATRICK. *(Wryly.)* You're a servant of the Lord, and I'm a servant of the servant of the Lord. *(Finishing.)* There now. Isn't that better?

CONRAD. Ohh my, yes.

PATRICK. Good.

CONRAD. *(Re: slippers but also glancing at PATRICK.)* Very handsome, indeed.

PATRICK. Yes, I liked them so much I took them in every color, but the black seems to suit you. And speaking of room service—what can I offer you?

(PATRICK takes CONRAD's shoes, stands and crosses to place them neatly beneath the luggage rack. CONRAD rises and walks around in a circle, getting the feel of the slippers, ending up down right.)

CONRAD. I really shouldn't have any more.

PATRICK. Not even coffee?

CONRAD. Well, I wouldn't say no to a coffee before I go.

PATRICK. I never say no to a coffee when I'm in Italy. It never tastes the same anywhere else in the world, I don't know why.

CONRAD. Well, you're a connoisseur. Man about several towns.

PATRICK. I'm just a country boy. Shucks, what do I know?

CONRAD. Some country boy! You like your Italian coffee in Italy, your French fries in France ....

PATRICK. *(A droll sigh.)* My Turkish baths in Turkey.

CONRAD. You say that so wearily.

PATRICK. I say that nostalgically. *(Changing subject.)* Now, about that coffee

CONRAD. *(Looks at his watch.)* You're sure you have the time?

PATRICK. I have nothing but time. That's why I invited you back. You said you like Sambuca?

CONRAD. *(Relenting.)* Yes, I do. I probably shouldn't have any more, but well, yes, an espresso will send me on my way. And a *liquore.* Is that how you say it?

(PATRICK starts to cross to the panel of service buttons on the stage left bedside table.)

PATRICK. *(En route.)* Sounds good to me. I'll ring for the floor waiter.

CONRAD. In a moment, if that's all right. *(PATRICK stops, looks at CONRAD. CONRAD moves back to the window. Re: view.)* I'd just like to take all this in a bit longer.

PATRICK. No rush. We'll just go *piano-piano.*

CONRAD. Did you learn to speak Italian just by being here?

PATRICK. Oh, I don't speak it. Even after years of coming here.

CONRAD. You did very well at lunch.

PATRICK. Menu Italian, that's all. I have no talent for languages. I put the sin in syntax.

CONRAD. *(Smiles.)* But it's obvious you have a talent for living. Thanks again for the extravagant meal! I like eating late. So long and leisurely. And for the drinks on the way back at the Caffè Greco.

PATRICK. Meals are included in the deal.

CONRAD. Lunch was on the brothers Warner?

PATRICK. *(Nods.)* Mmmm. And it cost them a *fortune*!

CONRAD. *(Chuckles.)* Well, I thank you anyway. You're very gracious and hospitable. You spare no expense.

PATRICK. It's almost impossible for me to do anything cheap. Almost. Especially with other people's money.

CONRAD. *(Laughs.)* God bless that expense account!

PATRICK. *(Grimly.)* Believe me, Father, it's small compensation for what one is put through.

CONRAD. Please. Call me Conrad. *(PATRICK doesn't respond. Expansively.)* Seriously, this has all been such a treat! And all in Rome. As close as you can get to heaven! The Holy City, the holiday, the high life!

PATRICK. A real summer cruise.

CONRAD. Oh, and am I dreading when the boat docks. I'll never forget this trip. It's made such an impression on me.

PATRICK. Funny how some things make an impression and others make no impression at all——like, do you remember where you were when Reagan was shot?

CONRAD. I must admit, I get excited by all these luxuries which seem to exhaust you.

PATRICK. Please, don't misunderstand. It's writing to the dictates of the committee that gets me down. It's the traditional, time-honored, fraudulent, formulaic bullshit of Hollywood that wears me out. Not what it can pay for.

CONRAD. *(Chuckles.)* No respect for writers or the written word?

PATRICK. Hollywood: nothing but brilliantly packaged lies.

CONRAD. Hollywood must package what it packages for a reason.

PATRICK. Lies sell tickets. Shit sells.

CONRAD. If it upsets you, why do you stay in such a profession?

PATRICK. I make a very good living selling shit.

CONRAD. You sound bitter.

PATRICK. *(Wryly.)* As bitter as that Campari you had before lunch. *(After a moment.)* Funny how everything you place your trust in turns around and dumps on you.

CONRAD. I hope you don't believe that's always the case.

PATRICK. Sorry if it sounds a tad self-pitying, but I think it's been the case for me.

CONRAD. I'd say it sounds more cynical.

PATRICK. I'm not ashamed of being cynical. I think being cynical is just being realistic. *(Sits on the edge of the bed platform with a heaviness.)* I must say, I'm bone-tired of the grind-of-it-all. Exhausted by the last go-round with this script. Believe me, it takes a velour slipper now and then to keep one's spirits up.

CONRAD. Of course, I don't know anything about how true show business is—but from the outside, it always *looks* and *sounds* glamorous.

PATRICK. I suppose it can be, but most of the time it's just like anything else—very hard work. People in the entertainment business work hard at putting on a show for those who've worked hard all day and need to be entertained. And them that totes the weary load see a show and look at all the so-called glamorous entertainers having what looks like a lot of fun. And these glum folks with their noses pressed against the glass think they're missing out on something—when all they're missing out on is the very thing they're sick and tired of— hard work. In the end it's a joke all the way round. Everyone working hard and, most of the time, not having much fun. And everyone fed up and longing for something that doesn't exist That's show business, and that's life.

CONRAD. You *are* cynical. But life can be wonderful. This day has been wonderful for me. And I wish it had been for you too. After all, we have a lot in common.

PATRICK. Such as?

CONRAD. When the weary come to me, I don't entertain them,

but I try to send them off refreshed ... and not with lies, of course, but with the truth.

PATRICK. There's a market for everything. You sell your brand of shit, and I'll sell mine.

(Silence. After a moment, CONRAD stands.)

CONRAD. May I indulge in my little vice?
PATRICK. What?

(CONRAD takes a pack of cigarettes from a side pocket of his jacket.)

CONRAD. May I smoke in here?
PATRICK. Of course.

(PATRICK gets up off the bed platform, goes to pick up an ashtray from the chest of drawers and crosses to CONRAD, placing it on the low table.)

CONRAD. *(Re: ashtray.)* Smoking in the restaurant—well, in that little enclosure of hedges on the street—that was one thing, but in your bedroom ....
PATRICK. Oh, I don't care. When in Rome ....

(CONRAD laughs. PATRICK takes a matchbook from the ashtray, lights CONRAD's cigarette.)

CONRAD. *(Re: the light.)* Thank you.
PATRICK. Living in L.A., I think it really would be hypocritical of me to get all bent out of shape about the quality of *air*.
CONRAD. Oh, but you know how people can be about secondary smoke. Actually, we're back where we started—fifty years ago we had to go behind the barn to do it, and that's where we have to go again!

(PATRICK goes to the bed to remove the paper from the wicker basket and gather up a few shirts. He crosses down left to open the top of the suitcase on the luggage rack and begins to pack them. CONRAD takes a long drag on his cigarette.)

PATRICK. Do sit down and make yourself comfortable. I'm sorry, but did you tell me why you're in town?

CONRAD. In town? You mean the *Vatican*?

PATRICK. And environs.

CONRAD. You know, there were times at lunch when I believe I completely lost your attention.

PATRICK. I apologize if I drifted off. Staring into space is one of my favorite things.

CONRAD. No need to apologize, you weren't rude at all. I just had the impression that sometimes we weren't really connecting.

PATRICK. Actually, my thoughts never left you for a moment—even when I got lost in them.

CONRAD. I hope you don't mind my saying so, you struck me the same way when I approached you on the street and spoke to you. You seemed to be just standing there in your own world.

PATRICK. *(After a moment.)* Yes, you sort of woke me up—I couldn't have written a better scene.

CONRAD. It *was* a bit like a movie, wasn't it?

PATRICK. Mmm. A real meet-cute.

CONRAD. A *what*?

PATRICK. Meet-cute. I suppose the classic example is when Claudette Colbert meets Gary Cooper shopping for pajamas. She only sleeps in the tops, and he only sleeps in the bottoms, so they buy one pair and split them. They meet-cute. And, it goes without saying, live happily ever after.

CONRAD. Ohh. And *our* scenario?

PATRICK. Let's see. Ohh, American religious, lost in the Holy City, looking for God or whatever—and along comes Godless

American, lost in his head, looking for God knows what.

CONRAD. *(Chuckles.)* I see. We met-cute.

PATRICK. Well, close but no pajamas. And who knows where the story goes from there.

CONRAD. Well, I, for one, hope we know each other happily ever after. Imagine! The first person I stop in that maze of little alleyways to ask directions was another American from Los Angeles who knows his way around like a native! What are the chances of that?

PATRICK. Slim.

CONRAD. Just imagine!

PATRICK. But the *world* is just a maze of little alleyways, isn't it? We might have bumped into each other anywhere.

CONRAD. Or we might not have.

PATRICK. Or we might not have.

CONRAD. Now that I've met you, Patrick, I do hate to think of that.

PATRICK. Who can fight fate? Now, remind me why you're here.

CONRAD. Well, actually I'm here on business, but it's been a lifelong dream to see this city. St. Peter's city—the rock upon which the church is built. But no harm in mixing a little business with pleasure.

PATRICK. Oh, yes, pleasure. I was focused for that part. And the business?

CONRAD. I'm attending a conference.

PATRICK. *(Groans.)* Ohh, conferences. I must have been staring into space for that part.

(PATRICK turns his attention to the laundry on the bed, goes to it.)

CONRAD. A series of lectures, actually.

PATRICK. Contraception, women priests, gay rights, that sort of thing?

CONRAD. *(Laughs.)* Well, not quite. Not yet!

PATRICK. Maybe on your next trip.

CONRAD. If I ever come back.

PATRICK. Maybe by then celibacy will be out and priests will be married. If that's their bent.

CONRAD. I must admit I'm more for tradition. I'm one of those who even wish it were all still in Latin.

PATRICK. Well, lots of luck and *Dominus Vobiscum.*

CONRAD. In my opinion, celibacy isn't going to go so easily. Because in many ways, I think it is a good thing.

PATRICK. Name one.

CONRAD. Well … it keeps a man from having to think about so many things that have nothing to do with his vocation.

PATRICK. Oh, come on, Father. Celibacy never stopped one human being from thinking about things he shouldn't be thinking about.

(CONRAD gets up, stubs out his cigarette in the ashtray on the low table and crosses toward PATRICK. PATRICK takes part of the stack of shirts and moves away from the right side of the bed before CONRAD reaches him. CONRAD studies the contents of the wicker basket. PATRICK crosses from the suitcase back to the left side of the bed, standing opposite CONRAD, and scoops up the rest of the shirts.)

CONRAD. Beautiful shirts. Like so many Easter eggs.

PATRICK. I try to get a little color in my life.

CONRAD. Beautifully finished.

PATRICK. They're brilliant at washing and ironing in this country. It's still done the old-fashioned way with such care and thoughtfulness, it's almost like forgiveness!

CONRAD. Extraordinary undershorts.

PATRICK. *(Smiles, crosses back to suitcase.)* They're lavish.

CONRAD. Silk?

PATRICK. Mmm, pure silk. *Seta pura.*
CONRAD. Italian, of course.
PATRICK. *(Nods.)* Local threads.

(PATRICK takes a handful of the silk shorts and goes back to the suitcase. CONRAD comes closer to the bed and extends a hand to finger the edges of a remaining pair of silk shorts.)

CONRAD. Custom made?
PATRICK. Just the shirts. The shorts are from the shirt maker's marvelous little haberdashery. Wonderful robes and scarves— *slippers,* of course, and … oh, I don't know, odd things.
CONRAD. Beautiful. *(CONRAD withdraws his hand as PATRICK returns and collects the rest of the shorts and transfers them to the suitcase. CONRAD turns and begins to slowly circle the sitting area of the suite, up right behind the settee. PATRICK closes the suitcase and goes to take the empty wicker basket off the bed and put it on the top of the chest of drawers. He looks up into the mirror to watch CONRAD as he takes out his pack of cigarettes, removes one, and lights it, stopping at the window to blow out the match and toss it over the balcony. He puts the pack in his inside breast pocket.)* The Italians really know how to do it, don't they?
PATRICK. They do indeed.
CONRAD. Wonderful style in everything.
PATRICK. They're really with-it about the general *presentation* of life. Which is *love,* I suppose.
CONRAD. *(Looks out at the city.)* Yes, it seems to be in the air here.
PATRICK. Sort of secondary, you might say. You just breathe it. Good for every organ.

(CONRAD laughs, turns back and goes to the ashtray on the lower table.)
CONRAD. *(Crushing his cigarette.)* Enough of this self-

pollution! I think I'll just get used to inhaling *amore.*

PATRICK. Ah, yes, *amore.* I suck up as much as I can.

CONRAD. That restaurant really did it with love. You could breathe that. It was palpable.

PATRICK. It was the garlic. A little too much garlic, actually. That restaurant really used to be much better. It's changed over the years. Like everything.

CONRAD. *(Jovially but a bit sadly.)* And every*one.*

PATRICK. *(Looking at CONRAD.)* Exactly. *(Turns to look at himself in a mirror.)* Getting old is the worst.

CONRAD. You're not old. *I'm* old.

PATRICK. *(Turns away from mirror.)* The truth is, I've always felt like I was never young.

CONRAD. Really? Why?

PATRICK. Ohh, my childhood was sort of short-circuited by … circumstances. *(Turns back to mirror.)* But now I can actually see myself falling to bits. It's the visual-of-it-all that's so disconcerting.

(PATRICK now turns from the mirror as if he cannot bear to look at himself. A pause. CONRAD goes to the window again and looks out.)

CONRAD. Things can be beautiful *because* of their age. Just look at this city.

PATRICK. When *I'm* three thousand years old, *I* should look so good! I heard an Englishwoman on the street the other day, looking up at the Villa Medici and saying quite forlornly, "It wants a coat of paint." *(CONRAD laughs pleasantly, looks at PATRICK, who again looks at himself in the mirror.)* I could use a coat of paint.

CONRAD. Are you talking about covering up the truth?

PATRICK. What's the point? Not worth it.

(CONRAD turns to study the view out the balcony window.)

CONRAD. *(Turns to PATRICK.)* I really don't know what I'd

have done if you hadn't come along this afternoon.

PATRICK. *(To CONRAD, thoughtfully.)* I don't know what I'd have done if *you* hadn't come along. Just carried on with my life in the same old way, I guess.

CONRAD. You didn't have any plans?

PATRICK. Still don't.

(CONRAD crosses to the armchair but does not sit.)

CONRAD. Surely you must have many friends here. Surely, you're not … well, you're not lonely. Are you?

PATRICK. Lonely?

CONRAD. For companionship.

(CONRAD takes a step toward the dressing stool. Then takes another. PATRICK immediately gets up and crosses in a slow straight line across the stage, up behind the settee, until he reaches the balcony.)

PATRICK. *(On the move.)* I'm never lonely when I'm in this city. Even when I'm alone. Even when I'm lost in a labyrinth of streets. This is one of my favorite places on earth. I've always felt secure here. Solo, but surrounded by love. I never feel more whole than when I'm in Rome.

CONRAD. I'm afraid there's a lot of the tourist in me. My first days here—whenever I was out alone and I heard someone speaking English, I'd always say hello.

PATRICK. I usually run for the nearest exit when I hear anyone speaking English.

(PATRICK turns from the window and crosses to the back of the settee, sits on it, one leg hiked up, facing CONRAD.)

CONRAD. But you didn't run when *I* spoke to you.

PATRICK. *(After a moment, directly.)* You interest me.

CONRAD, You're an intriguing fellow yourself, Patrick.

PATRICK. *(Flatly.)* I'm strange. And I know it.

CONRAD. *(Chuckles.)* I think all of us are stranger than we let on.

PATRICK. I'm stranger than you'd think, Father.

CONRAD. You'd never know it to look at you.

PATRICK. Or to look at *you. (CONRAD laughs uncomfortably.)* I told you, what you see is what you *don't* get. It's all just show. If I were turned inside out, *you'd* run for the nearest exit.

CONRAD. *(Sits on the arm of the armchair.)* Now, that's hard to believe.

PATRICK. I'm as creepy as the creepiest person you ever saw on a street and wouldn't dare ask directions even though you were hopelessly lost.

CONRAD. Why do you usually run from people when you hear them speaking English?

PATRICK. Don't like the familiarity, I suppose.

CONRAD. You hear so much about fear of intimacy these days. Self-help books, TV talk shows, the Internet.

PATRICK. *(Dryly.)* Everything but semaphore. *(CONRAD laughs. PATRICK moves to the window, looks out.)* Solitude not only makes me content, in some strange way it exhilarates me. *(After a moment.)* Even in the American cities I've live in, I'd sometimes get in a taxi or get in my car and go to parts of town that were foreign, so to speak. Unfamiliar territory. And when I finally traveled to real foreign towns in real foreign countries, I felt that familiar, safe freedom of being a stranger in a strange place. I *wanted* to be lost. I didn't *want* to understand what was going on. And whenever I'd learn the language a little, I'd move on. To other countries with more difficult, more arcane languages which I could not possibly pick up. I tried that in Finland, once. Forget it.

CONRAD. Maybe that's why you've never learned the language in this country.

PATRICK. Yes, I don't want to spoil it for myself. I don't want to be disappointed by the banality of it all. I prefer the mystery. In my hometown, there were these wild Sicilians I adored but whose lingo I resolutely refused to pick up. A widow and her three children who became sort of my surrogate family. Of course, I always felt like a fifth wheel, but it didn't matter. They were so full of life—just a great big cliché, really—lots of loud and passionate squabbling, lots of tears, lots of love ... and, of course, lots of *pasta*.

CONRAD. Which was reassuring.

PATRICK. Exactly.

CONRAD. It's a wonder you don't prefer Palermo to Rome.

PATRICK. Palermo is *too* Sicilian! Palermo is meshuga! *(CONRAD looks blankly at PATRICK.)* Pazzo! Crazy!

CONRAD. Why were the Sicilians your surrogate family? Your parents were there for you, weren't they?

PATRICK. Well, they weren't there for each *other,* so, yeah, they were all over *me* like the mange.

CONRAD. What do you mean? I don't mean to pry.

PATRICK. *(Wave of the hand.)* Far niente. I just mean, divorce was out because of the Church, so I was a kind of excuse to keep their unhappy marriage together. I was coddled and coached and clocked to be a success, because my success would be *their* success. Of course, the stakes were so high, I was like something let out of a burning barn! I guess I would have flipped out for good if it hadn't been for the Sicilians and for ....

CONRAD. Someone special who got you through? A teacher?

PATRICK. No, not a teacher—the movies. That bright ray of light from a projection machine very definitely dazzled me. It offered hope ... and a way out.

(Silence. A slight pause.)

CONRAD. I felt that way about the priesthood.

PATRICK. It offered a way out?

CONRAD. I think so.

PATRICK. A way out of what?

CONRAD. Ohh, life. As I knew it. My family life, I suppose. That, and I wanted to be in touch with man's suffering. I wanted to make a difference. When I was in school and a priest passed through the playground, there were no more fights, no more resentments. The face of the nastiest kid became angelic, everything changed. At least, for me. Oh, there are so many reasons why I became a priest.

PATRICK. Personally, I'd have only done it for the robes.

CONRAD. The vestments?

PATRICK. I used to be crazy about dressing up as an altar boy— all that lace! It made me feel above the congregation.

CONRAD. Ritual is a powerful thing.

PATRICK. And it gives power.

CONRAD. Yes … but, when I was young, I felt ….

PATRICK. What? Powerless?

CONRAD. Well … incomplete. Fragmented. Not whole. The love of God and some contact with Him seemed to be the one thing that gave me strength. I remember when I was an altar boy … one morning no one showed up for six o'clock mass, and when the priest gave me communion—just to me and no one else—I never felt so special. I felt so ….

PATRICK. What? Powerful?

CONRAD. Well, I found something that gave me the strength to pull myself together and have hope. It almost made me sick with joy to know that devotion afforded a way out.

PATRICK. Was your family religious?

CONRAD. My father died before I knew him. But my sister was, although she was quite a bit older; I never knew her much until I had to move in with her while I finished high school. Just before I went into the seminary.

PATRICK. Why did you have to move in with her? Did your mother die too?

CONRAD. Oh, no. I just couldn't live with her anymore. Things were just too … tense … and, well, unhappy.

PATRICK. Your mother wasn't a religious person?

CONRAD. Yes and no. She was like anybody else, I suppose—you know, commit … transgressions … and then go to confession, get absolution, and do her penance. She always said going to confession made her feel like a brand-new human being. Of course, as soon as she got home she would start all over again.

(CONRAD takes a handkerchief out of his outside breast pocket and starts to wipe his hands.)

PATRICK. What's the matter?

CONRAD. Oh, nothing. My mouth is just dry.

PATRICK. *(Looking at CONRAD's action.)* And your hands are wet.

CONRAD. *(Laughs, chagrined.)* Yes! So they are!

PATRICK. Are you ready for the *caffè*?

CONRAD. Oh, my, yes! And maybe a little *acqua minerale*.

PATRICK. There's some beside the bed. Help yourself.

CONRAD. *Grazie. (PATRICK goes to press the service panel on the night table stage left of the bed. Lightly.)* Maybe we should have doubles! I must be putting you to sleep.

(CONRAD puts the handkerchief back in his breast pocket.)

PATRICK. On the contrary. I'm riveted.

(CONRAD goes to the night table stage right of the bed and pours some mineral water into a glass, drinks it and replaces the glass on the tray. PATRICK closes the suitcase, snaps it securely.)

CONRAD. Are you packing to leave?

PATRICK. In he morning.

CONRAD. *Really?* I don't know why, I got the impression your work on the movie was going to keep you here much longer. I thought that's why you "drifted off" in the restaurant—I thought you were thinking about your work.

PATRICK. No, my work, such as it is, is finished. *(Looks at CONRAD.)* Give or take a loose end or two. And you're here just till the end of the week? Then it's back to Los Angeles and to teaching?

CONRAD. Why? Do I look like a teacher?

PATRICK. Yes, you do.

CONRAD. Well, I did teach once, but I don't anymore. Now I'm ....

PATRICK. Why is that?

CONRAD. *(Evasively.)* Oh ... it's a long story.

PATRICK. Do you miss it? Teaching.

(PATRICK settles on the dressing stool.)

CONRAD. I do. I always got a great deal of satisfaction out of it. Seeing them learn and grow up and go out in the world. It made me feel I'd touched their lives.

PATRICK. It must have filled you with a great deal of pride.

CONRAD. Oh, it did. Because I was crazy about it—doing what I really wanted to do. And it went beyond the classroom. I had a nice car, and I'd pick up the kids and we'd drive to the country, take hikes, swim, have pillow fights, and I'd let them stay up as late as they'd like. There was nothing like helping those boys to believe in themselves, because a lot of them were from troubled backgrounds and really didn't know ....

PATRICK. Love?

CONRAD. *(Nods.)* They really didn't know what it was to have anyone take an interest in them. Oh, we had some terrific times!

PATRICK. They must have worshiped you.

CONRAD. Oh, it was so rewarding. For them. For me. *(Adds, lightly.)* Of course, I'd always let them win!

PATRICK. You sound like you were just a big kid yourself.

CONRAD. Maybe so. Sometimes I got into trouble with my

superiors because I was rather lax with the paperwork.

PATRICK. The grown-up stuff.

CONRAD. Yes, you might say that. Kids never give a damn about paperwork.

PATRICK. You don't deal with them at all anymore?

CONRAD. No.

PATRICK. That must be very hard on you.

CONRAD. Now I'm chaplain in a hospital. For a while I was in school administration—picking out textbooks, that sort of thing. Then I did a short stint as an adviser to Catholic charities. Then when parish work didn't pan out, I became a chaplain.

PATRICK. What hospital?

CONRAD. Oh, I move around a lot within L.A. Go where the job is. *(Lightly.)* Kinda like being in show business, I would imagine.

PATRICK. *(Not responding.)* You must deal with a lot of AIDS.

CONRAD. What?

PATRICK. People with AIDS.

CONRAD. Oh, well, naturally. *(Changes subject.)* Anyway, the only thing I was really good at was teaching. I enjoyed it. *(Thoughtfully.)* Yes, I enjoyed it so much. *(Slight pause.)* And you? Back to L.A? Or is it New York?

PATRICK. Both, eventually. First, I'm going to stop in London and have a meeting with a producer. I have a play in mind, and he's offered to put it on if I can just write it.

CONRAD. If you can just write it?

PATRICK. Yes, I've had this play in mind for years, but I can't seem to get at it.

CONRAD. Not enough time?

PATRICK. Oh, no, not that. The famous writer's block.

CONRAD. The creative process! It's always fascinated me.

PATRICK. And eluded me.

CONRAD. Do you have any idea as to why you're blocked?

PATRICK. Well, I know I'm only blocked when it comes to writing something personal. Something of my own. So that's why I'm in Hollywood selling shit.

CONRAD. What a pity that you can't get in touch with your true feelings.

PATRICK. It's hard, don't you think, getting in touch with your true self?

CONRAD. Maybe I'm blessed, but I don't know that I've ever had that problem.

PATRICK. Oh, well then you *are* blessed.

CONRAD. Oh, I may have had a crisis—a spiritual crisis in my time, but I've always managed to pull through. I think prayer saved me. I'm very devoted to the Blessed Mother. What a pity you can't ….

PATRICK. Ask Her to get me out of the fix I'm in? Place my faith in God?

CONRAD. I think you already have faith, Patrick, no matter what you say.

PATRICK. *(Shrugs.)* Faith is personal and easily misunderstood.

CONRAD. God understands.

PATRICK. *(Sardonically.)* You can swear to that on a stack of Bibles?

CONRAD. There are so many issues on which the Church seems adamant, but … well … I mean, there is an official position, of course, and these days particularly I have to take that position in the pulpit, but there can be mitigating circumstances.

PATRICK. You can bend the rules to stay in the club?

CONRAD. Well, no, but for instance, in the context of one couple to one counselor regarding, say, contraception … we can ….

PATRICK. Do lunch.

CONRAD. Well, there is always the official versus the unofficial.

PATRICK. Just a tad hypocritical around the edges, isn't it?

CONRAD. *(Defensively.)* Well, life is not black-and-white! Life, I'm afraid, is endless shades in between!

PATRICK. *(Controlled.)* You're talking out of both sides of your mouth!

CONRAD. *(Mounting ire.)* Talk about hypocrisy after what

you've said about your profession as a writer!

PATRICK. I don't defend *my* profession!

CONRAD. It's the same in all institutions, religious and secular!

PATRICK. *(Drolly.)* Yeah, who's ever heard of a politician who's even masturbated.

(CONRAD is somewhat embarrassed, and the moment is defused.)

CONRAD. *(Covering his discomfort.)* If I had your quick wit, just imagine the sermons I could write!

PATRICK. Would you practice what you preached?

CONRAD. *(Getting back to the original subject.)* At lunch you told me you've written very personal work in the past.

PATRICK. Oh, yes, I've bared my soul, so to speak. All fired up with ambition and productivity. And I don't understand how I did it one bit. I think if I can ever rediscover my imagination, I'll find myself.

CONRAD. Imagination can be more revealing than the truth.

PATRICK. Exactly. I once had an analyst in Beverly Hills who never wanted to hear the mundane particulars of my daily life. She'd say, "Just bring me a big, fat, juicy dream." *(CONRAD laughs.)* Anyway, I have an idea for a play—I know how it starts now, how it progresses up to a point—it's kind of a dream.

CONRAD. A big, fat, juicy one?

PATRICK. Mmmmmm. Quite tasty.

CONRAD. But you don't know how the dream comes out yet? Is that it?

PATRICK. Well … it's getting there.

CONRAD. What's it about?

PATRICK. *(Avoiding the question.)* You know, when I was a child I could draw picture after picture and never get tired or bored or exhaust my imagination. At Christmas I could wrap gift after gift—each different, more charming, more original. And when I started to write, I was tireless at writing sketches and playlets and, finally, plays one after another. But I cannot write plays anymore. Not even the one floating around in my head. Why can't plays come out of me like pictures and presents?

CONRAD. In my own way, I know what you mean. In the hospital, I find it very difficult to counsel grieving families. It's one thing to console the dying but quite another to know what to say to the living! Because when someone dies, those left behind feel ... responsible. How do you give them hope and strength to go on? I'm afraid that's something not in my power. What are you thinking?

PATRICK. I hope we both find our way.

CONRAD. We'll find a way. I know we will. If we just go *piano-piano*.

PATRICK. From you mouth to God's whatever, Father.

CONRAD. Conrad. Your friend.

PATRICK. Conrad.

(Silence, for a moment, which is broken by the room service WAITER unlocking the door with his keys. He enters. He is about PATRICK's age.)

WAITER. *(Entering.) Permesso.*

PATRICK. *Si, avanti.*

WAITER. *Prego, signori?*

PATRICK. *(To CONRAD.)* Coffee and a *liquore*?

CONRAD. That would be very nice.

PATRICK. Do you want Sambuca, or would you like to try something else?

CONRAD. You mean like grappa?

PATRICK *(To WAITER.)* Do you have Genepy?

(Note: Genepy is pronounced in English and Italian GEN-a-pee.)

WAITER. I will ask the barman downstairs.

PATRICK. If so, we'll have that. And two coffees.

WAITER. *Due* Genepy. *Due Caffè.*

PATRICK. *Solo uno* Genepy *e due caffè, per favore.*

WAITER. *Grazie. (PATRICK goes to retrieve the laundry basket and hands it to the WAITER.)* Everything was nice and clean?

PATRICK. *Si, si. Era limpida come la pipi di un' bambino.*

(The WAITER laughs wickedly and goes out.)

CONRAD. I couldn't understand that, but from the way he laughed, it must have been something dirty.

PATRICK. Not really. Just an expression. I said everything was as clear as baby piss.

CONRAD. *(Chuckles.)* What is Genepy?

PATRICK. Something from the Dolomites. Made from juniper berries. Rome's a little far south to have it.

CONRAD. I'm sure a hotel like this has everything. But even I understand enough Italian to know you didn't order one for yourself. You said, "*Solo uno* ..."

PATRICK. I don't drink. That is, I don't drink *anymore.*

CONRAD When you refused the wine this afternoon, I thought maybe you just didn't imbibe at lunchtime.

PATRICK. I used to imbibe at lunchtime, cocktail time, dinnertime, and stay up all night and sing 'em all! Now ... I don't *drink* at all. Or, rather, I struggle not to. I'm an alcoholic. And alcoholic blocked writer—how's that for original?

CONRAD. An *ex*-alcoholic.

PATRICK. Well I'm what we call in the program a "recovering" alcoholic.

(CONRAD stands, takes his pack of cigarettes from his side pocket and lights one. CONRAD moves to look out the window.)

CONRAD. If you ever had a serious drinking problem, I think you must be some kind of miracle.

PATRICK. There you go getting religious again.

CONRAD. But these twelve-step programs are all about spirituality.

PATRICK. Yes, and that's not to be confused with religion. Religion is what people get when they're afraid of going to hell. Spirituality is what they get when they're on their way back from there.

(CONRAD laughs.)

CONRAD. Are you on your way back?

PATRICK. I'm in transit.

CONRAD. If you're ... agnostic, what do you make your Higher Power?

PATRICK. The group.

CONRAD. The power of the collective.

PATRICK. For me it's the humanity of the group. There's something very poignant about the *humanity*. And very compelling. Something about the frailty of a group of vulnerable human beings, struggling valiantly against their darker instincts.

CONRAD. I wouldn't have any problem whatsoever turning myself over to God. I never have—and you wouldn't either, if you saw what I see in a hospital. Yes, you were right.... I see so many who die of AIDS.

PATRICK. I thought you must, but you didn't seem to want to talk about it.

CONRAD. I don't know why I didn't before. *(After a moment.)* Anyway, there was one young man whose family rejected him. He was near the end, and I came by to give him what I still call Extreme Unction and was shocked to find him in the best spirits I'd ever seen! He said it was because, at last, his friends had come to say good-bye. The room was empty, and he was blind, so I asked, rather carefully, who was there. "Don't you see—there's Violetta and Lucia and Mimi." Well, I don't know the first thing about opera, but he introduced me to the three of them and said, "You know, I'm blind, but I can really see them, so this must be a miracle." And I said yes, it sure is, and took it as a sign that it was time to give him the last rites. When, suddenly, he sat bold upright and gasped some strange word— "*Ree-na-chee*!"—and then, fell back on the bed as dead as dead can be. Well, after all *that*, I didn't need a drink. I needed the comfort of God. And I went to the chapel, and I prayed. Prayed for that young fella's soul. The whole *idea* of a power higher than myself was very comforting to me.

PATRICK. *Rinasce.*

CONRAD. I didn't know what the hell he was talking about.

PATRICK. Violetta's last line in *La Traviata*. She's Italian, so naturally she goes on a bit longer. *"In me rinasce,* yadah, yadah, *oh, gioia*!" It means, "In me, there is rebirth. Oh, joy!"

(Pause.)

CONRAD. I suppose you know a lot about opera?

PATRICK. No, I don't. What I know a lot about are those long, long intermissions. I always enjoyed them so much more than I did the opera itself. It was my favorite time to get shit-faced on champagne. And I didn't even *like* champagne! I much preferred the comfortable haze of the first dry martini.

CONRAD. You only went to the opera to drink between the acts?

PATRICK. To get drunk, really.

CONRAD. Well, there must have been a less expensive way.

PATRICK. Well, yes, but as you put it about praying to God in the chapel—the whole *idea* was comforting to me, the romance of it all, the glitz, the glamour—long-stem glasses and more than a bit of the bubbly in a splendid crush bar or some dead-assed Founders' Circle. That and a lot of *posing,* no doubt. *Heavenly.* Except when it turned hellish.

CONRAD. *(With private interest.)* It could turn on you?

PATRICK. Could, and finally did. I once flew to Paris with a friend for *La Bohème* on Christmas Eve. Well, now, the very *idea* of an opera taking place on Christmas eve and seeing it that very same night, and *Paris*, and *Puccini*, and the *interminable* intervals, and all the chilled champagne in the whole of France was too much for me! I drank so excessively after the first act that I passed out and snored all through the Café Momus scene in the second. Then woke up and threw up. Ruined my new dinner jacket. My friend had to get me up the aisle and out. By this time, I was singing along. Needless to say, I was not a hit at the Paris Opera. And my friend hasn't forgiven me to this day.

CONRAD. Talk about "bottoming out" in style!

PATRICK. Oh, so you know about bottoming out, do you?

CONRAD. *(Quickly.)* Well, I know what's meant by it. *(Moving on.)* I envy you. In your own way you've redeemed yourself. In the end, I hope I'm redeemed. And delivered.

PATRICK. Are you guilty of something?

CONRAD. Who among us is not?

PATRICK. Is that why you've come to Rome?

CONRAD. Of course not. But it is inspiring here. I feel … cleansed here.

PATRICK. *(With an edge.)* Purged?

CONRAD. That's a good word.

PATRICK. *(Heating.)* Absolved? Pure as silk? Clear as baby piss?!

CONRAD. *(Evenly, but with an effort.)* You penetrate with words, Patrick. It's obvious you're a writer.

PATRICK. And an ex-Catholic. Guilt is an old friend of mine. As the joke goes—the Jews may have invented guilt, but the Catholics perfected it.

CONRAD. *(Testily.)* You're not an ex-Catholic, you're a fallen-away Catholic.

PATRICK. *(Adamantly contrary.)* Maybe I should say, a *recovering* Catholic.

CONRAD. *(Not conceding.)* But once you are baptized, you are always a Catholic! *(Flippantly.)* Something like being an alcoholic, isn't it?

PATRICK. *(Sarcastically.)* Once a Catholic, always a Catholic. Once a priest, always … safe.

CONRAD. *(Testily.)* I'm not ashamed to say God keeps me safe—that the priesthood is, for me, like a haven.

PATRICK. *(Tauntingly.)* Like a cover?

CONRAD. *(Thrown.)* A cover? *(Forced lightly.)* You mean like a security blanket or like ….

PATRICK. *(Bluntly.)* I mean like a *mask*. Like something to *hide* behind.

CONRAD. *(Heatedly.)* Now, just one minute, my son.

PATRICK. *(Snidely.)* I am not your son, Father.

CONRAD. But I am still a priest.

PATRICK. And a priest is still a human being! He's still a man, and the church is no haven, no "safe house" in which a man can hide out from temptation.

CONRAD. *(Pointedly.)* No, and in order to resist the more insidious temptations of this world, most human beings place their faith in God! In the end you'll believe in God. Mark my words, you'll call out for Him, and it's going to be such a powerful epiphany, your tongue is going to rot in your mouth!

PATRICK. *(Bitterly.)* In the end, this fugitive from the premises of God only prays he has the courage to meet the unknown and die without screaming for a priest!

CONRAD. *(Violently.)* Enough of this!

PATRICK. OK! *Basta. (Slight pause. Silence. Deliberately.)* I once heard someone say in a meeting that the three requisites for being alcoholic were, one—being an orphan, two—being a survivor of child abuse, or three—being a Catholic. I thought they had a point. I qualify on two of those counts. I am not an orphan.

(CONRAD is silent. The sound of a key enters the lock. The door opens, and the FLOOR WAITER enters.)

WAITER. *Ecco, signori*!
PATRICK. *(Re: liquore.)* Ah, you *do* have Genepy!
WAITER. I have brought you the whole bottle!
PATRICK. *Bravo*!
WAITER. *Salute*!

(The WAITER sets the tray on the low table.)

CONRAD. *(Crossing.)* May I have a look at the label?

(PATRICK picks up the bottle of liqueur and hands it to CONRAD, who studies it as PATRICK takes the bill from the WAITER.)

CONRAD. What a color! As green as your eyes, Patrick.
PATRICK. Help yourself.
CONRAD. Thank you. I do want to try it.

(CONRAD opens the bottle and begins to pour himself a pony of Genepy as PATRICK signs the bill.)

PATRICK. Among its other powers, it's great as a *digestivo*.
CONRAD. Then it's heaven-sent.
PATRICK. *(To WAITER, handing him the bill.)* Grazie.
WAITER. *Prego, signor. Grazie a lei. Buona sera.* *(Deferentially.) E buona sera, Padre.*
CONRAD. *(Nods pleasantly.)* Buona sera. *(The WAITER goes out. PATRICK follows him to the door as CONRAD tastes the Genepy. Re: liquore.)* Oh, my, that is delicious. *(Aspirates.)* But strong! My God!
PATRICK. *(Rolls his t's in mock exaggeration.)* Forte! Forte! *(Suggestively.)* It'll put starch in your collar, Padre. *(CONRAD is a bit thrown by the vulgarity of the remark but laughs feebly.)* Just put on a Roman collar and people automatically have respect for you, don't

they?

CONRAD. Or contempt.

PATRICK. Does that happen in America the way it does here? I mean that little tacit courtesy?

CONRAD. Sometimes.

PATRICK. Anyone could dress up in that costume and get respect, couldn't they?

CONRAD. Or contempt.

PATRICK. Sometimes contempt can be more exciting than respect. Too much respect can be paralyzing. *(PATRICK has picked up the espresso pot and poured two cups.)* Sugar?

CONRAD. Just black, please. *(PATRICK hands CONRAD a demitasse.)* Thank you. *(CONRAD takes his cup and sits on the left end cushion of the settee. PATRICK goes to sit on the right end cushion, then hesitates a moment before deciding, instead, to turn and settle into the armchair. Re: espresso.)* I need this. *(After a moment.)* I really shouldn't drink, either. One or two's my limit—three tops.

PATRICK. Just to put the stopper on, so to speak?

CONRAD. Well, I will admit I used to be able to handle it better. I just have to exercise a little more control these days.

PATRICK. Control's always a good thing to exercise. Control and one's abdominals.

CONRAD. *(Smiles, pats his stomach.)* Oh, no dinner for me tonight! Just very early to bed. *(Re: Genepy.)* I'll be ready after this. Delicious.

PATRICK. *(Re: Genepy.)* Yes, I have fond memories of it.

CONRAD. It's not a problem if I drink this in front of you?

PATRICK. You could swing from the chandelier if we had one, and it wouldn't faze me.

CONRAD. You mean you never even think of it anymore?

PATRICK. Oh, it's always on my mind—like death.

CONRAD. *(Laughs, sips Genepy. After a moment.)* Do you know why you drank?

PATRICK. To get some feeling going. And to stop any feeling.

CONRAD. Can you run that by me again?

PATRICK. It all boiled down to that—to fill one's system with *anything*—anything just to stop *feeling* something—or anything to *feel* something.

CONRAD. *(Reflectively.)* I see you've given this some thought.

PATRICK. Sometimes I wanted to feel as bad as I could and would smoke or snort or swallow anything to make me feel just as rotten as possible because, at least, I *felt something*. To feel *bad* is, at least, to *feel*.

CONRAD. I grew up with a family of drinkers. Working-class people from Ireland. Both my parents were big, big drinkers. My father used to say he didn't trust a man who didn't drink. You've heard that one.

PATRICK. *(Dryly.)* Yes, and from no one I admire.

CONRAD. My father was banned from every pub in Galway, no mean achievement. So he came to America and started all over.

PATRICK. Do you know what an Irish queer is? A fellow who prefers women to drink.

(CONRAD laughs hollowly. There's a slight pause.)

CONRAD. My father died of cirrhosis when I was just a boy, and although my mother died years later of heart failure, it was all brought on by years of drinking too. Slow drinking. I somehow wish she'd gone first. It would have spared me so much ... so many .... *(Breaks off.)* It's one reason I think I went in the priesthood as soon as I could.

PATRICK. What is?

(Slight pause.)

CONRAD. *(Rationalizing.)* She was a good person, basically. But, like anybody—human. With human flaws. *(Directly.)* Forgive me for rattling on. I don't know what got me started.

PATRICK. Tell me more. Dump the cargo and fly low.

(CONRAD smiles, takes a deep sip of Genepy.)

CONRAD. It's something I never talk about—my family. My mother.

PATRICK. Why's that?

CONRAD. *(Forced lightly.)* I suppose you might say I'm blocked.

PATRICK. It's not easy being a numb.

(Silence. CONRAD takes another sip of Genepy.)

CONRAD. *(After a moment.)* Let's just say my parents weren't happy people.

PATRICK. That's something we have in common.

(CONRAD is silent, takes an even bigger swig of Genepy.)

CONRAD. *(Motioning to Genepy.)* May I? *(As PATRICK nods.)* It's really and truly funny to think of us both as blocked.

PATRICK. Well, not *too* hilarious

CONRAD. You're a bit of all right.

PATRICK. Am I?

CONRAD. You're a "cozy" person—like the dark snug of a pub. I feel I've known you forever.

PATRICK. Maybe it's my Southern charm.

CONRAD. You're from the South?!

PATRICK. Is the Pope celibate?

CONRAD. But you don't have an accent.

PATRICK I had one once that you could cut with a sugar cane machete.

CONRAD. Sugar cane … let's see—Louisiana?

PATRICK. Mississippi.

CONRAD. *(Stunned.) Mississippi*?! You're *joking*! You didn't tell me that at lunch!

PATRICK. I was too busy impressing you with all the celebrities I've known.

CONRAD. But I assumed you were from New York!

PATRICK. No.

CONRAD. Where in Mississippi?

PATRICK. Oh, just a little cow track.

CONRAD. Well, that *is* interesting.

PATRICK. *(After a moment.)* Is it? Why?

CONRAD. Well … for one thing, you certainly don't sound it. I'd never have guessed. How did you get rid of your accent?

PATRICK. I was a speech and drama major in college—and I took lessons to get rid of it.

CONRAD. Whatever for? Southern accents are so charming.

PATRICK. I thought a regional twang made one sound like a hick. Appear stupid. Of course, that's just what I was—a stupid hick. But I didn't want to sound like one! *(Pensively.)* Also ….

CONRAD. Yes?

PATRICK. I saw it as kind of failure. Something imposed on me without my consent. One *more* thing, I should say. *(Deliberately.)* I once felt that way about my homosexuality.

(Slight pause. CONRAD tries not to appear thrown by PATRICK's remark. CONRAD reaches for the Genepy bottle and pours himself another drink.)

CONRAD. *(A bit uncomfortably.)* You didn't tell me that, either.

PATRICK. I didn't think I had to.

CONRAD *(Lightly.)* If you'd drunk as much of that Pino Grigio as I did, Patrick, I'd say it was the vino talking now. But, then, all you had was mineral water.

PATRICK. So maybe it's just the gas talking.

CONRAD. *(Laughs nervously.)* Con gas! That's about all the Italian I've picked up. *Acqua minerale. Con gas o senza gas!*

(CONRAD chuckles feebly at his own joke. PATRICK doesn't. Silence. CONRAD rummages nervously through his pockets.)

PATRICK. Have you lost something?

CONRAD. I ... I ... *(Quickly.)* I don't know what I did with my cigarettes. *(Gives up search.)* It doesn't matter. Better if I don't find them, anyway.

PATRICK. They're in your left side pocket.

CONRAD. You'd make a good detective. *(CONRAD takes out the pack of cigarettes as PATRICK picks up the matches and strikes one. CONRAD puts a cigarette in his mouth, and PATRICK gets up and lights it for him.)* Thank you.

PATRICK. *(After a moment.)* Didn't it cross your mind?

CONRAD. What? No. It didn't.

PATRICK. Really?

CONRAD. *(After a moment, lightly offhanded.)* You certainly are very candid.

PATRICK. There's no point in being anything else. It takes too much effort to lie. All that keeping track of the "official" story. Not worth it. Unless, of course, I get paid for it.

CONRAD. Well, telling the truth is indeed a great virtue. *(PATRICK is silent. CONRAD takes another long swig of Genepy, then becomes more serious.)* You say you considered your ... sexual proclivity ... some kind of failure?

PATRICK. I guess I did. I tried to get rid of that too.

CONRAD. And you didn't succeed?

PATRICK. Well, let's just say, the attempt was less successful than with my accent. I knew I was gay from the time I was six, and I wasn't very happy about it. But I no longer feel that way.

CONRAD. If *I* may be candid ... exactly how did you try to go about getting rid of it? Your ... homosexuality. Therapy of *another* sort?

PATRICK. Exactly.

CONRAD. The psychiatrist in Beverly Hills?

PATRICK. *(Turns to CONRAD.)* Psychoanalyst. She was one of several. All women. Most all of whom were of some note. Maybe I should have dropped their names at lunch too.

CONRAD. You do everything first rate.

PATRICK. As I said, it's almost impossible for me to do anything cheap. *Almost.*

CONRAD. *(Expansively.)* Of that, I'm convinced!

PATRICK. So far I've simply chosen to tell you one side of the story. The safe side. The cozy, snug side. I don't think you'd want to hear about my nostalgia for the gutter. The cheap side. However, in its way, that was always first-rate too, inasmuch as you couldn't get any lower.

CONRAD. I doubt that I'd be shocked. I've heard a lot in my time.

PATRICK. In confession?

CONRAD. Well, yes, of course. But I *am* a man of a certain age. I may have been born yesterday, but I wasn't born *late* yesterday.

PATRICK. *(Laughs.)* I like that. I think the Genepy has knocked the edges off.

CONRAD. *(Raises his glass of Genepy.)* Cheers!—And *buona notte!* *(PATRICK doesn't laugh, just looks at CONRAD. Slight pause.)* I know a priest who works with homosexuals.

PATRICK. "Works with"? That sounds arduous. Like it might even smart.

CONRAD. There are some, Patrick, who would like to reconcile themselves with the Church.

PATRICK. And what if they just can't pretend they're something they aren't?

CONRAD. Well, off the record, and admittedly it's becoming more difficult, but I suppose if there's a consensual, nurturing, monogamous relationship ....

PATRICK. You can work out a deal. Forgive me for saying the

obvious, but who wants to be a member of that cockamamie club? *Cockamamie*—That's Yiddish too.

CONRAD. *(Chuckles.)* Why do you keep using Jewish words? You're not Jewish.

PATRICK. I might as well be—show business and psychoanalysis are my life!

CONRAD. Of course, Jesus was Jewish.

PATRICK. No, he wasn't. He was Irish.

CONRAD. What?

PATRICK. Consider the facts—on the last night of His life, he went out drinking with the boys. He thought His mother was a virgin, and she thought that He was God.

CONRAD. *(Laughs, holds up glass.)* What's the name of this?

PATRICK. Genepy.

CONRAD. Genepy. Great stuff. I wouldn't have missed it for mass! *(Looks heavenward.)* Just kidding, Lord! *(Another slight uncomfortable pause. CONRAD gets up, goes to he balcony window, looks out, and sips his Genepy thoughtfully.... After a moment.)* Whoever said "small world" really knew what he was talking about!

PATRICK. What do you mean?

CONRAD. *(After a moment.)* I once taught school in Mississippi.

PATRICK. Now, that's something you didn't tell *me*.

CONRAD. I'm telling you now.

PATRICK. Why didn't you mention it before? When I said I was from Mississippi.

CONRAD. *(Evasively.)* Well ....

PATRICK. Well, what?

CONRAD. *(Uncomfortably.)* Well, suffice it to say I *did* teach there. Isn't that another unbelievable coincidence?

PATRICK. *(Casually.)* Small world. Enormous fate, I guess.

CONRAD. Amazing!

PATRICK. Life *is* ... *amazing* sometimes.

CONRAD. Yes, imagine! Each of us now living in the same

random American city, never knowing the other existed within that city or state or space—and having also existed within another state and space at the same time, sometime in our pasts. And now, our paths cross in a distant, foreign place! What are the chances of that?!

PATRICK. Slim.

CONRAD. Of course, I'm not from L.A. originally. I'm from ....

PATRICK. *(Evenly.)* Boston would be my guess.

CONRAD. *(Dumbstruck.)* You do have a sharp ear for accents! And I never even said, "I pahked the cahr in the Hahvahd yahd!" *(CONRAD laughs at his own joke. PATRICK does not.)* Actually, I'm from South Boston. I'm a "southie." Went to seminary outside Brookline and taught for a while in Beverly, Mass. Then I was sent to one of our schools in Mississippi.

PATRICK. And how did you wind up in L.A?

CONRAD. *(Evasively.)* I was ... unhappy ... in Mississippi ... in that small town, so I asked to be transferred to a city. Any city anywhere that needed someone. I needed to be ... swallowed up. *(Re: Genepy.)* May I?

PATRICK. But of course.

(CONRAD refills his glass, takes a long sip. Pause. CONRAD takes another sip, looks to see PATRICK staring at him.)

CONRAD. You're so silent. You're not falling asleep, are you?

PATRICK. I'm not even staring into space.

CONRAD. What are you thinking? *(PATRICK looks at CONRAD a moment longer, doesn't answer, gets up, and goes to the window to look out.)* Something you don't want to say? *(PATRICK is silent. After a moment, CONRAD gets up and crosses to stand beside him. Silence. Some street noises. Someone somewhere is singing and whistling a snatch of "Non Dimenticar." Pause. Looking out.)* Ah, bella Roma! The Eternal City.

PATRICK. *(Looking out.)* Maternal, paternal, eternal.

CONRAD. What a fantastic night. I've always preferred the night. The night always exaggerates things—there's a kind of heightened reality, isn't there?

PATRICK. Yes, it's like drink or a drug. I was a night person too, all my life. I used to feel alive only at night. Now I quite appreciate the day. There's nothing more beautiful than light—and what it does to things. Light and shadow are something to consider. I envy painters.

(CONRAD puts his hand on PATRICK's shoulder and looks out at the city.)

CONRAD. This has all been so extraordinary, I shall never forget it. Meeting you. Becoming friends. Imagine—just hours ago we were two strangers in a foreign country.

PATRICK. I have always been a stranger in a foreign country— always. There and then as a child in the South—and here and now in this Holy City. Excuse me.

(PATRICK gently slips out from CONRAD's grasp, moves away, crossing to the back of the settee, where he sits, his back to the audience. CONRAD doesn't leave the window, but turns from it to face PATRICK.)

CONRAD. What's the matter, Patrick? Don't like being nostalgic?

PATRICK. I'm a person who dwells on yesterday to the point of pathology.

CONRAD. In some cases I think it's better to forget and move on.

PATRICK. The past, for me, is not a darkened stage whose players have vanished and are forgotten.

CONRAD. *(Almost as if he's seeking advice.)* Do you really

think you can resolve the troublesome things of the past?

PATRICK Some things. But it's hard to confront the big time.

CONRAD. *(Re: the Genepy.)* You know, it's really *Kelly* green!

PATRICK. *(Drolly.)* You mean it's user-friendly.

CONRAD. *(Warily.)* Did you go to Catholic school in Mississippi?

PATRICK. Mmm. I wonder if you can guess which one.

CONRAD. Well, there are so many! Isn't it amazing how many Catholic schools there are in a hard-core Baptist state? *(Picking up the Genepy bottle.)* May I have a tiny drop more?

PATRICK. Be my thirsty guest. I not only went to Catholic grade school and high school but even a Catholic university. My father was rather cracked on the subject of religion.

CONRAD. And your mother?

PATRICK. Oh, she converted just to keep peace. She only went to church on Sundays to show off her fur coat.

(PATRICK gets up, moves away to the chest of drawers. He starts to place the toilet articles—cologne and talcum—into the zipper case lying on the top of the chest.)

CONRAD. *(Settles into the armchair.)* The older I get, the more I find myself doing things just the way my mother did.

PATRICK. Such as?

CONRAD. Ohh, little things like ... tucking my handkerchief in the sleeve of my cassock or checking things several times before I can go out—the light in my room, the front door, the back door. Sometimes I lock and unlock and *re*lock the doors three or four times before I can leave.

PATRICK. Just as she did.

CONRAD. Yes. *(Hesitantly.)* And in the last couple of years I've noticed something else—something I hated as a child—something I never thought I'd be doing.

PATRICK. Like?

CONRAD. Like … taking to bed in the middle of the afternoon when I've always been so on the go, so active. I've always hated lying around. But sometimes I get depressed—just like she used to get depressed.

PATRICK. What about?

CONRAD. Things I thought I'd left behind so many years ago in South Boston.

PATRICK. And why did you leave? Mississippi, I mean. Not Massachusetts.

CONRAD. *(Carefully.)* As I say, I was transferred.

PATRICK. You said you *asked* to be transferred

CONRAD. Yes, that's right. *(Lightly.)* Are you taking this down?

PATRICK. I'm a good listener, Father

CONRAD. You certainly are.

PATRICK. And an even better scopophiliac.

CONRAD. What's that?

PATRICK. The morbid urge to observe. You were saying?

CONRAD. I came to love the South, but … well, it got to be too ….

PATRICK. What? *(Playfully.)* Too humid? Too hot?

CONRAD. *(Seriously.)* Too painful … for me to stay there. *(With a certain difficulty.)* I had a bad experience—got myself into a … troublesome situation there, so it was somewhat of a relief to get out.

PATRICK. Then it *did* get too hot for you?

CONRAD. *(Tonelessly.)* Well, you might say that.

PATRICK. And sticky?

CONRAD. *(Grimly.)* Yes. I guess you might say ….

PATRICK. The heat was on?

CONRAD. Believe me, it was no joking matter.

PATRICK. I believe you *(Pause. CONRAD puts down the coffee cup on the low table, picks up the pony of Genepy and drains it. He pours himself another, settles back in the armchair. After a moment.)*

What's the matter, Conrad? Are *you* nostalgic now?

CONRAD. *(Evasively.)* Just very mellow. This Genepy is making me very, very sleepy. I must get up and stretch. *(Stands, yawns.)* Ohh my, your bed looks so inviting. *(PATRICK looks at CONRAD reflected in the mirror. He doesn't turn to face him. CONRAD puts down the empty Genepy glass on the low table and comes up to the left head of the bed.)* The sheets! Real linen, are they?

PATRICK. Mmm. I love that about good hotels in Europe.

CONRAD. *(Extends his hand.)* May I?

PATRICK. Go ahead. Give it a feel.

CONRAD. *(Touches the pillow.)* Soft and smooth— *(CONRAD then sits carefully on the bed. Reacting to the comfort.)* Oh, my! How luxurious. I'd better not go any further or I could curl up and spend the night!

PATRICK. Could you?

(CONRAD slightly bounces up and down on the mattress.)

CONRAD. I could indeed.

(There is the sound of a key in the door as the FLOOR WAITER returns.)

WAITER. *(Entering.) Permesso.*

PATRICK. *Sí, avanti.*

(CONRAD immediately gets off the bed.)

WAITER. Are you finished with the tray?

PATRICK. We're finished with the coffee.

(The WAITER crosses to the low table.)

WAITER. I will leave the Genepy.

PATRICK. Thank you.

WAITER. *Mi scusi*, Padre, you like the Genepy? *(Picks up bottle, looks at contents.)* Oh, I see you like it very much.

CONRAD. Yes, it's very soothing.

WAITER. It is good in the wintertime—for "after-ski."

CONRAD. Well, you might say I've been going downhill all afternoon! *(The WAITER doesn't really understand but smiles enigmatically and refills CONRAD's glass. He sets the bottle on the low table and picks up the tray with the coffeepot and used cups and starts to go.)* Grazie.

WAITER. *Grazie, a lei, Padre. Buona sera.*

CONRAD. *Buona sera.*

WAITER. *(To PATRICK.) Buona sera, signor.*

PATRICK. *(Pointedly.) Grazie et buona notte.*

(The WAITER goes to the door. CONRAD goes back to the low table and picks up the drink as PATRICK comes around the bed and follows the WAITER out. PATRICK casually locks the door [three revolutions] and puts the key in his side jacket pocket. CONRAD's back is to PATRICK, but he hears the sound of the door being locked. Whether he thinks anything of it or not, he doesn't react or comment on it. PATRICK doesn't move from the door. CONRAD goes to the window. Some car horns are heard from below and a few indistinct exchanges in Italian. A Vespa goes by. Pause. CONRAD turns to face PATRICK, who is looking at him.)

CONRAD. *(After a moment.)* What are you thinking?

PATRICK. I'm thinking about your sitting on my bed.

CONRAD. Oh, I hope you don't mind, it just looked so ....

PATRICK. There was a time—not so very long ago, Conrad— that I'd have taken that as a come-on—if someone had come up to my room and patted my pillow and asked to give it a feel.

CONRAD. *(Lightly.)* Now, really, Patrick, are you trying to shock me?!

PATRICK. I'm not saying what was on *your* mind. I'm just telling you what was going through *mine.*

CONRAD. I just meant that … well … what I mean is, I'll definitely take a little nap as soon as I get back to my room. *(Looks at his watch.)* —and I really have to think about going.

PATRICK. *(Looking at the bed.)* The difference between then and now is that I'd have been drinking like you've been drinking this afternoon. Half-pissed and horny, I'd have picked up someone in a bar or off the street or in a pissoir and probably paid them. That would have been the first-rate gutter side of me. But not anymore. Those days are over. I'm too sober. *(Grimly.)* And the world's too sober today too. The leaves are knee-deep in the pissoirs in the Borghese Gardens now. Sign of the times.

CONRAD. You know, Patrick, sometimes you go a bit too far.

PATRICK. It could have been an afternoon like this afternoon, Conrad. After all, I did sort of pick you up on the street, too, didn't I? And brought you back here with me?

CONRAD. *(Admiringly intrigued.)* You just don't care what you say, do you?

PATRICK. I just don't think there's any point in pretending *(Shrugs.)* Not worth it.

CONRAD. Actually, I wish I were like that. I admire people who say what they think. People who have that power.

PATRICK. You mean it's a tough for you to let down your hair. Expose yourself?

CONRAD. I don't think anything would shock you.

PATRICK. It'd take some doing. Try me.

CONRAD. You mentioned something earlier that made me think of something in my past. It's been on my mind ever since.

PATRICK. What has?

CONRAD. I don't know what telling you would accomplish. I've never spoken to anyone about it. *(Waves his glass.)* What is this, anyway?

PATRICK. Jet fuel.

CONRAD. *(Lightly.)* You're going to have to roll me out the door and point me in the direction of the Tiber! And even then, I'm still bound to get lost. *(Re: Genepy.)* What *is* it, anyway? I know you say it's made from juniper, but it's like ....

PATRICK. Truth serum! In juniper veritas!

CONRAD. *(Sits on the settee.)* I believe you may be right. *(After a moment.)* You've made me think of things that really have always been just out of mind. *(After a moment.)* Funny, I feel so light-headed.

PATRICK. Take a few deep breaths and just go *piano-piano.*

CONRAD. *(Chuckles.)* Yes. That might help.

PATRICK. It helps me.

(CONRAD is silent. A slight pause.... PATRICK sits on the foot of the bed. CONRAD sits next to him.)

CONRAD. *(Breathing heavily.)* As I say, I've never talked to anyone about this, and I don't know if I'm prepared even to tell you. I'd like to.

PATRICK. *(Carefully.)* Would it help if you thought of me as you, well—as your ... father confessor?

CONRAD. Are you being ....

PATRICK. Tongue-in-cheek? No, for once.

CONRAD. *(Tentatively, re: liquore.)* I think this ... this Genepy has loosened my tongue.

PATRICK. Do you always have to drink to loosen up?

CONRAD. Well, it always helps.

PATRICK. And are you relaxed now? Are you comfortable with me?

CONRAD. Yes. You certainly know how to put a man at ease.

PATRICK. Thank you.

CONRAD. You have that power.

PATRICK. Thank you again.

CONRAD. Power must be the most intoxicating thing in the world. Far more heady than alcohol.

PATRICK. Maybe there's just something about me that encourages you to be intimate.

(A loaded pause.)

CONRAD. *(Anxiously moves away.)* I don't think I can. Speak of it. I'm sorry. Been bottled up in me too long.

(Silence. A pause. CONRAD silently sips the Genepy. PATRICK gets off the bed.)

PATRICK. *(Flatly.)* I doubt if you could tell the truth about yourself to anyone.

CONRAD. *(Somewhat startled.)* What?

PATRICK. You have done nothing but pretend to me since I met you. Pretend to be chaste, pretend to be celibate. And yet you sit on my bed and make seductive remarks. You can be had, Conrad.

CONRAD. What did you say?

PATRICK. Too intimate for you?

CONRAD. I don't know what you mean!

PATRICK. And you're a drunk! That's one's choice, of course, but you lie about that too—pretending "one or two's my limit—three tops!" You have no limit. There is no top. Boundaries are a problem for you, Conrad.

(CONRAD is unsettled, knocks over the glass of Genepy on the low table, and looks up with apprehension.)

CONRAD. *(Flatly.)* Patrick, you're way out of line!

PATRICK. *(Drawing nearer, quietly.)* You're a failure at everything you set out to be—a teacher, a shaper of young minds, the bearer of the word of your God. With your lies you have betrayed the integrity of a tradition centuries old. You're a flop as a priest. You're a flop as a person. Conrad, you are a *flop*.

CONRAD. And you are something evil!

PATRICK. If I am, I am your creation, dear Father!

CONRAD. What are you talking about?!

PATRICK. *(After a moment, directly.)* I have a confession to make concerning that play that I can't seem to get at. It's about a betrayal of trust. Emotional betrayal. Sexual betrayal.

CONRAD. *(Standing, anxiously.) Give me my shoes!!*

PATRICK. What's the matter, don't you like being in mine?!

CONRAD. I'm leaving!

PATRICK. I'm not finished telling you about the play.

CONRAD. I don't think I'm interested!

PATRICK. It's about a teacher who sexually abuses a nine-year-old student.

(Pause. CONRAD stands silently aghast, staring wide-eyed at PATRICK.)

CONRAD. *(Hisses weakly.)* Who are you?!

PATRICK. *(Calmly.)* Don't you know? I loved you once.

CONRAD. What?

PATRICK. I said, I loved you once.

(CONRAD's jaw sags with recognition.)

CONRAD. *(After a long moment.)* It's not possible!

PATRICK. Apparently, it is. *Very* small world department!

CONRAD. *(Quickly.)* His name wasn't Patrick!

PATRICK. Yes, it was! His middle name was Patrick, but you

called him by his first name. You called me ….

CONRAD. *(A hushed gasp.)* Ned!

PATRICK. Yes. You called me Ned. Ned for Edward, which is my first name. Just like my father. You remember my father, of course.

CONRAD. Your father?

PATRICK. Your friend, *Eddie!*

CONRAD. *(Remembers.)* Of course, I remember your father. Dear, kind Eddie. How … how is Eddie?

PATRICK. Dead. So he's just fine.

CONRAD. *(Compassionately.)* I am sorry to hear that. We were great friends. I liked Eddie so much.

PATRICK. And he was impressed with you. Bright young Irish-American priest. What he probably always wanted to be himself.

CONRAD. Eddie probably did think he missed his calling. Yes, I suppose he did look up to me.

PATRICK. He'd do anything for you. Give you anything. Anything you wanted. And you *wanted* the things my father could give you. You loved the perks. The cigarettes. The liquor. The good wine. The gifts of money. The car. The Christmas-of-it-all!

CONRAD. I didn't ask for those things!

PATRICK. You didn't have to. My father was generous, and in that small town he thought you were special. Educated, cultivated, and *holy*! A man of God. Good for his boy. And how did you pay him back? By molesting his son!

(CONRAD runs to grab his shoes from under the luggage rack. PATRICK races after CONRAD and snatches his shoes from him and hurls them across the room. CONRAD, suddenly terrified of PATRICK's unbridled wrath, collapses back onto the top of the closed suitcase on the luggage rack.)

CONRAD. *(Hysterical.)* Why have you come back?! To get even?

PATRICK. *(Hovering.)* Ask your all-knowing God that! Ask Him why, after all these years, He's permitted this curious little collision in the mad mix-up of streets in this ancient holy town!

CONRAD. Let me go! Let me out of here!

(CONRAD starts to get up and PATRICK shoves him back onto the suitcase.)

PATRICK. And while you're at it, ask Him why He permitted you to sit beside me at my desk in the middle of a room of prepubescent students and put your arm around me and slip your hand down the sides of my overalls to fondle my ....

CONRAD. Stop it! Stop it!

PATRICK. Why He allowed you to slip my hand into your cassock where your trousers were unzipped.

CONRAD. *(Covering his ears.)* Stop! Don't do this!

PATRICK. Why He let you take me to your room after class to kiss me and suck me and have me kiss and suck you.

CONRAD. Please, for God's sake!

(CONRAD pushes past PATRICK, races for the door. PATRICK doesn't move. CONRAD begins to tear at the knob.)

PATRICK. *(Calmly.)* It's locked. Didn't you see me lock it when the waiter left? *(Removes key from his pocket, holds it up.)* Here's the key.

CONRAD. *(Rushing back to PATRICK.)* Give it to me!

PATRICK. *(Calmly puts the key back in his pocket.)* No.

CONRAD. *(Pathetically.)* Give it to me. Please.

(CONRAD breathes hard, backs away from PATRICK, stumbles on the raised platform and falls onto it [downstage of the foot of the bed], panting. PATRICK looks at CONRAD contemptuously.)

PATRICK. *(Icily.)* You look a bit green around the gills. As green as that Genepy you've been lapping up. *(Calmly.)* I remember a day, a day of dread and anxiety the likes of which I have never known again—although at nine years of age I didn't know what the unnamed thing in me was. I wonder if you remember that day?

CONRAD. *(Breathing hard.)* What day? What are you talking about?

PATRICK. *(Without affect.)* A cold day one winter when you were colder than the day outside. I knew something was wrong the moment I saw your face that morning. The moment you looked away from me and never looked at me again. I thought I had done something. I thought something was *my* fault. I couldn't eat at the lunchtime recess—the smell of sausage in the cafeteria made me ill. I couldn't play in the playground. I couldn't even see clearly, even though there wasn't any bright sunlight—just a canopy of gray, that chilly, dull noon. All I could do was wonder and worry and wait for the bell to come back to class … when you finally spoke to me. Without looking at me you told me to stay after school—that you had something to talk to me about. What had I done? What had I caused to make you so cold?

CONRAD. You didn't understand.

PATRICK. The hours dragged by like days that day of dread until, at last, at three o'clock on that cold, dreadful afternoon, the school bell rang again and the rest of the students left, leaving me alone with you. And you locked the door.

CONRAD. Please, I want to forget—

PATRICK. You remember there was a mesh grating over the windows in that room—

CONRAD. Yes … yes, I remember.

PATRICK. And I remember how that day the mesh seemed like a cage to me. The moment you started talking, I wanted to get out of that room. I was going to suffocate. I asked you to unlock the door, and you said, "No, I have to talk to you." *(PATRICK crosses to bed platform, stands over CONRAD and addresses him directly. CONRAD avoids PATRICK's gaze.)* You didn't sit beside me at my desk this time—you sat on the one in front of me—you didn't touch me, you kept your distance. You couldn't look at me when you finally said, "What we have been doing has to stop. What we have been doing is wrong. What we have been doing is a sin." Do you remember?

CONRAD. *(After a moment.)* Yes. Yes, of course. How could I forget?

PATRICK. You unlocked the door and let me go. And I've never felt free again. After that—the hours, the days left in that year—the interminable anxiety of having to be near you in the classroom, hearing your voice day after day. Seeing you in the schoolyard at recess, playing with the other children—running into you on the stairs, in the corridors, never having our eyes meet again, never knowing what was going on in your mind. Then, coming back after the summer and suddenly finding out you were gone. Disappeared. They said you'd been transferred. I never knew where, never knew what happened to you, never heard of you again. Until this day.

CONRAD. I can't believe this day!

PATRICK. Believe it. You're good at putting your faith in things which stretch credulity far more than this day. Such is life and show business in a bewildering world.

(PATRICK moves away, crossing unsteadily to lean against the back of the settee. CONRAD slowly gets up off the platform, begins a slow semicircle downstage around PATRICK, edging right to search for his shoes. The next exchanges are rapid-fire.)

CONRAD. *(Moving.)* How long have you been following me?

PATRICK. I haven't been following you!

CONRAD. You followed me here to Rome, didn't you?

PATRICK. No, I didn't.

CONRAD. You tracked me down, haven't you?

PATRICK. Running into you was just what it was—an accident.
A sort of *divine* accident!

CONRAD. You planned this!

PATRICK. I had no plan! But I do now.

*(CONRAD has edged his way down left. He finds his shoes, picks
them up, goes to sit in the armchair, takes off the slippers.
PATRICK slowly comes around the settee and up to the
armchair, to loom over CONRAD, who finishes pulling on his
shoes, leaving them unlaced. CONRAD panics and runs to the
balcony as a Vespa grinds past on the street below, making a
racket. PATRICK doesn't move from the door. The sound of the
Vespa loudens....)*

CONRAD. *(Yelling outside, over the noise.)* Help! *HELP!!!*

PATRICK. *(Without passion.)* The word in Italian is *aiuto! Aiuto!*
It means "help." *(After a moment.)* What's the matter? Can't you say
it? *(CONRAD is frozen with fear, unable to utter a syllable. We hear
the rasp of the Vespa fade in the distance. PATRICK calmly crosses to
the balcony, steps around CONRAD, and closes the exterior shutters,
then the glass doors, shutting out the exterior noises. He then draws
the brocade portieres. CONRAD stumbles dizzily back to center stage,
starts to moan and contract his arms about his midsection. He
collapses on the floor. Turning tonelessly.)* Get up.

CONRAD. *(Moaning.)* I can't.

*(PATRICK calmly crosses to stand above CONRAD but does not
touch him.)*

PATRICK. I said, *get up!*

(CONRAD starts to gasp and crawl across the floor toward the

bathroom door.)

CONRAD. I'm sick!
PATRICK. What's the matter? Choke on your rosary?

(CONRAD moans loudly, grabs his stomach with one hand and covers his mouth with the other, as if he is about to vomit. He gets to his feet and stumbles the rest of the way across the stage into the bathroom.)

CONRAD. I'm going to be sick!

(We hear CONRAD retch offstage. PATRICK slowly approaches the open bathroom door, looks in. After a moment, he speaks.)

PATRICK. *(With mild contempt.)* Pity. All that expensive expense-account lunch down the toilet. *(The sound of the toilet being flushed can be heard offstage.... PATRICK steps across the threshold to the bathroom, where he can still be seen by the audience, whips a towel off the warming rack and hurls it off to where CONRAD would be. PATRICK steps back over the threshold, into the room. The sound of running water is heard offstage.... Suddenly, PATRICK pulls the bathroom door shut and collapses against it, hyperventilating. He stands there gasping a few seconds, then forcefully pushes himself away from the door, propelling himself around, stumbles to center stage, where he stops, frozen for a moment, before he begins to shake violently.... Desperately, to himself.)* Pat, Pat, Pat, Pat, Pat, Paddy, Paddy, Paddy .... *(He gasps for breath.)* Neddy, Neddy, Neddy, Ned, Ned, Ned, take a few deep breaths ... take a few deep breaths .... Hold on ... hold on ... hold on .... *Piano-piano ....* (A pause. He calms. And straightens. And smoothes his hair.... The sound of the running water in the bathroom is turned off. After a moment, the door to the bathroom is thrown open and CONRAD staggers out, looking* *ghostly pale. He has taken his suit jacket off and clutches it in his hand. His hair is wet and a towel is around his neck.... CONRAD moves unsteadily to hold on to the chest of drawers. He looks up at himself [and at PATRICK] in the mirror. PATRICK becomes aware of the eye contact, turns away to look straight out front.... After a moment.)* Do you recognize me?

(CONRAD does not turn around—continues to look at PATRICK in the mirror.)

CONRAD. I didn't at first. You're older, of course.... But now .... *(Turns to face PATRICK.)* Well, yes, you are unmistakably you—

(CONRAD turns back to the mirror, takes the towel from around his neck and wipes his face, picks up PATRICK's comb and smoothes his hair. He puts down the comb and the towel on top of the chest.)

PATRICK. *(Turns to face CONRAD.)* Even before I saw you, I knew. I heard your voice when you spoke to me, and I knew. Then I looked at you, and even behind dark glasses, I knew—
CONRAD. I'm older too. My hair ... it's all salt-and-pepper—
PATRICK. Not to worry. There's still more pepper than salt. *(Out front, simply.)* I've seen your face in so many people through the years. Someone will look up and see me staring at them—on a plane or in a restaurant or a theater, and they'll never know that I wasn't looking at them at all. I was seeing you.
CONRAD. *(Not looking at PATRICK.)* Even though you're a grown man now, you still have the same sweet face, Neddy.
PATRICK. Don't call me that!!
CONRAD. That's who you are.
PATRICK. No. That's who you want.
CONRAD. *(Weakly.)* I've got to lie down.

PATRICK. *(Coolly.)* You've been wanting to get in my bed since you got here, haven't you? *(CONRAD stumbles to platform, steps up on it and falls onto the bed.... PATRICK goes to his suitcase, flings the top open and scoops up all his pairs of silk boxer shorts. He crosses to the bed, mounts the platform and stands over CONRAD, pelting him with the undergarments....)* Here. You've been wanting these too. Hold them. Feel them. Smell them.

CONRAD. *(Shrieks at PATRICK.)* You can't even it out! For God's sake, Ned!

PATRICK. I said, *don't call me that!*

CONRAD. All we can do is repent for the unthinkably monstrosity of what happened ....

PATRICK. *(Lashes out.)* Of *what you did*! Not *what happened*. There is nothing even in what happened! We're talking about the unspeakable monstrosity of *what you did*!

CONRAD. Do you blame me for everything that's gone wrong with your life?

PATRICK. Do you have any idea how you changed my life?! And I don't mean you made me homosexual. I mean, do you know how you fucked with my mind?! *(CONRAD doesn't respond. PATRICK turns to him. Directly.)* Well, *do you*?!!!

CONRAD. I have paid for what I did!

PATRICK. You've *never* paid for what you did!

CONRAD, *(Directly.)* How would *you* know! You don't know me. You don't know the way I've had to live my life. *(Hysterically.) You don't know the secrets of my heart!*

PATRICK. *Then SHOW me your heart if you have one*!

CONRAD. *(Lashes out.)* What do you want me to do?! I've confessed, I've been absolved, I've done my penance. I've begged God over and over and *over* for forgiveness!

PATRICK. *(Confronting CONRAD.)* I am the only one who can forgive you! *I* am the child you violated!

CONRAD. *(Looking up at PATRICK, terrified.)* What are you

going to do?!—*What?*—Hurt me?!

PATRICK. *(Calmly but steely.)* Sorry, no bamboo shoots under the fingernails!

CONRAD. *(Stoically.)* Are you going to kill me?

(PATRICK straightens, very controlled, turns, and moves a little way left of CONRAD.)

PATRICK. Hold a linen-covered pillow over your face until you suffocate? Push you off the balcony and have you splatter your guts all over the Spanish Steps? Too predictable. No, this scene will not be written by the dictates of a committee. This scene will be of my own invention. *(CONRAD gets up and runs for the door and begins frantically twisting the knob. PATRICK crosses to him, catches him by the back of his collar and swings him round. CONRAD swings round and drops to his knees, center stage, sobbing.)* Listen to me!

CONRAD. *(Covers his ears.)* No!!

PATRICK. *(Takes him by the lapels, shakes him.)* I said, listen to me, goddamnit!!!

(CONRAD tries to crawl away from PATRICK's grip. PATRICK jerks him around so forcefully that PATRICK himself is brought to his knees. CONRAD screams. Now they are both kneeling, face-to-face, CONRAD down on both knees, cowering—PATRICK on one knee only, slightly higher and above CONRAD, in the stronger position with more physical advantage. CONRAD sobs as PATRICK tightens his grip on CONRAD's jacket lapels....)

CONRAD. Patrick, I'm an old man!!

PATRICK. A *dirty* old man! A filthy old pervert in a costume!

CONRAD. I'm a man of God!

PATRICK. Then ask your God why He permitted you to be the first person to teach me what I thought was love?! *Love!* For the first time in my life! And for the last time in my life!

CONRAD. What are you saying? You didn't want me to end it?

PATRICK. You should never have begun it! What has love meant to me ever since? Humiliation and betrayal. I can have sex with strangers, but I can't make love with anyone who could love me or for whom I could feel one authentic emotion. And for that, I have you to thank.

CONRAD. I had to end it! It was wrong!

PATRICK. At the moment you told me it was wrong—that it was what you called a sin—at that moment you taught me the meaning of guilt.

CONRAD. Mother of God, I never meant to hurt you!

(CONRAD struggles with PATRICK. PATRICK stands, violently pulls CONRAD to his feet and hurls him across the room onto the bed, pinning him down.)

PATRICK. You wrecked me inside forever! I was left with nothing but apathy, indifference, a detachment toward everything that is given any emotional credence in this world. The thought of a human being about whom I might genuinely care makes me ill. It makes *me* want to vomit. And left with that numbing emptiness, I fill it with a pathological commitment to luxury, a life of living beyond my means, an obsession for expensive, inanimate possessions of quality which cannot betray me. That is why I want nothing more than for my life to end. Certainly I want nothing after it is over. I despise the idea of your God. I want you to live with that knowledge. I want you to live knowing that you are responsible for the *death of a soul of a human being.*

(PATRICK releases CONRAD, steps off the platform, and walks away to center. A pause. CONRAD weakly lifts himself up on his hands on the bed and looks at PATRICK.)

CONRAD. *(After a moment.)* I often wondered if you'd even remember.

PATRICK. *Remember*!

CONRAD. I thought it might be something so shameful that you'd force yourself to block it out forever.

PATRICK. It doesn't work that way!

CONRAD. *(After a moment he looks at PATRICK.)* Did you tell your father?

PATRICK. I told my mother.

(Slight pause.)

CONRAD. What did she do?

PATRICK. Nothing. I think she was afraid to tell my father. But she didn't go to anyone else—your superior, for instance. She did nothing. All she said was, "That dirty old son of a bitch. I always knew he was freaky."

CONRAD. I thought about getting some treatment. I knew it was something dark for which I needed help, but it seemed easier to bury it. We should never do anything with the hope of forgetting. *(After a long moment.)* The irony is, it happened to me. That's what I wanted to speak of but couldn't. What was so difficult to admit a few minutes ago now seems like nothing. I was abused. All my young life. By my mother. *(PATRICK looks at CONRAD.)* After my father died, she made me share the same bed with her until I finally took it upon myself to get out and go live with my sister. I couldn't endure the … tension of it anymore, the cat and mouse of it … the unspoken *fact* of it. In the winter months we'd sleep spoon fashion, and I remember one night when I was twelve years old, lying there I felt the warm satin of her nightgown pressed up against me, rubbing me. I began to get excited, and I got an erection. At first, I didn't know whether she was asleep or not, but after a while … after she let me almost reach the point of ejaculation she reached behind herself and pushed me away—I knew she knew. I turned over, facing away from her ... and I .... This went on time after time, year after year, nothing was ever said—even though the sheets would be circled and slightly discolored the next morning.

PATRICK. It explains something, I suppose. Not enough. But something. But so what? Is that supposed to make what you did to me all right? It hasn't made me do it. It hasn't made me even think about doing it.

CONRAD. I never did it again either. If you can believe it— never with another child after you. Ever!

PATRICK. I don't know that I *can* believe it.

CONRAD. There've been adults.

PATRICK. Teenagers?

CONRAD. Consenting *adults*!

PATRICK. In California, the age of consent is *eighteen.*

CONRAD. You were the only child! The only one!

PATRICK. If that is true, it's a privilege I could have lived without.

CONRAD. I know that doesn't make it any less wrong—any less my fault!

PATRICK. No, it doesn't. Because *you* were an adult. I was a child.

CONRAD. Yes. A bright child. A seductive child. Alluring and dangerous. You were like a little spark of divinity, tinged with a shadowed side, some inner sadness, a melancholy I recognized and wanted to fix by touching you, holding you, making it all right. I could never get over how long you could sustain eye contact with me. You were never shy. You never looked away. You were bold.

PATRICK. Oh, I see. So *I* was the source of temptation! All children are seductive, but they are *children.* They are not the ones in control!

CONRAD. Yes. Yes, I know. I know better than anyone that

children are helpless.

PATRICK. What did you think about what you were doing?

CONRAD. I knew it was risky. I knew it was against the laws of God and man, but at the time I must not have considered anything except … the excitement.

PATRICK. You didn't consider the consequences?

CONRAD. They made me sick with fear.

PATRICK. The consequences to *you.*

CONRAD. And to *you.* I never told anyone about it, except some unknown priest in a confessional. I finally got up the nerve and drove to New Orleans—no one would know me there. I didn't tell him that I was a priest, only that I was a teacher. He said he would grant me absolution only if the sin were never, ever repeated.

PATRICK. *(Snidely.)* And you felt like a brand-new human being.

CONRAD. I can still hear his voice. He said the sin was mortal— that if I continued, I would be excommunicated, denied the sacraments, forbidden all contact with Holy Mother Church. He asked me if I thought I was fit to be a teacher and suggested I find another profession—remove myself from the near occasion of sin—the company of children. I promised I would, and he absolved me. On the drive back I was in a stupor, but I knew I had to speak to you the next day and somehow get through the rest of that term. Leaving abruptly would've caused a scandal. When that year was finally over I asked to be transferred and prayed that would be the end of it.

PATRICK. *(Sarcastically.)* A simple moral failure, according to the club. Something calling for penance and plain old willpower. So it's five *Hail* Marys and out of the door for ten *Bloody* Marys! It would have been far worse if you'd have slept with a woman. That would have meant you'd broken your vow! *(CONRAD, in an attitude of exhaustion, slowly, heavily swings his feet to the floor but doesn't seem to have the strength to get off the bed. Looking off right.)* You were a decent man, Conrad. Do you know why you did it?

CONRAD. *(Looking off left.)* I have no idea. The whole thing is something I've never understood. Why I did what I did to you—why I did what I did to myself. Teaching was my calling ... and I ruined it. Now I am a minister to the comatose—giving sacraments to people who don't now if they're in this world or the next, let alone that I'm standing there, praying for their salvation. It's an empty task to say empty homilies over and over and over to a congregation that's long since stopped listening. Now, I'm surrounded by death. And when I think of my own death approaching, I don't even have my faith to comfort me.

PATRICK. All I want is to resolve the past so that I can go on, go on to God knows what. It's a joke, but some mysterious part of me wants to love and be loved—wants it in the mildest, most removed but most insistent way. In the end, none of it makes sense. Nothing tracks.

CONRAD. Like having met the way we did after all these years. It's all a mystery.

PATRICK. Exactly. *Pazzo.* Meshuga.

CONRAD. What I did is something I'll never forget or get over or comprehend.

PATRICK. You can try, and all you'll get is a giant explosion, like the first blast of the universe. Something you simply cannot explain. In the end, whatever you figure out, whatever you really crack, just reassembles into a question mark as soon as you turn your head.

(Silence. A pause. PATRICK goes upstage center, takes the key out of his pocket and unlocks the door [three revolutions] and leaves the key dangling in the latch. CONRAD slowly gets off the bed. PATRICK slowly moves downstage right, facing away from CONRAD as he goes to the door and stops....)

CONRAD. *(At the door, after a moment.)* I want to ask something of you.

PATRICK. *(Not turning, facing out.)* What is it?

CONRAD. Would you please … put your arms around me? Hold me for a little moment?

PATRICK. *(Not looking at CONRAD, after a moment.)* I wouldn't be at all interested in that.

CONRAD. *(Resigned.)* I understand. *(CONRAD opens the door. PATRICK hears the sound of the latch opening but still does not turn. CONRAD opens the door, starts to go, stops, shuts the door and turns back. ...)* Will you …. *(PATRICK's body reacts to CONRAD's voice, having assumed that the sound of the door closing meant CONRAD had departed. ... Begs.)* Will you please forgive me?

PATRICK. *(After a moment.)* I don't know.

(CONRAD slowly comes beside PATRICK and kneels down beside him.)

CONRAD. *(Quietly, begging.)* I want to atone for my sin. I want to be good—to be clean. Forgive me. Only you can make me clean. Make me—after all these years—pure. Restore me. Make me whole I beg you. *(PATRICK doesn't respond. CONRAD takes PATRICK's hand, presses it against his forehead.)* I confess to Almighty God and to you, my son, that I have sinned against you. Forgive me, Patrick. Forgive me, Ned. I beg you to forgive me.

(A church bell begins to toll somewhere in the distance. ... The sound is faint, as the doors to the balcony are shut.)

PATRICK. *(After a moment.)* I … I … forgive you. *(After another moment, absently.)* Go in peace.

CONRAD. God bless you.

(CONRAD kisses PATRICK's hand. PATRICK does not pull away. CONRAD lets go of his hand, gets off his knees and goes to the door. PATRICK does not look at CONRAD as he opens the door

and leaves, closing the door softly behind him. A beat, as the church bell continues to toll. PATRICK turns toward the muffled sound, goes to the window and, with his two hands, whips the portieres apart and pulls open the balcony doors. Suddenly, a surreal blaze of white light incandesces the room from outside as a strong wind blasts inside, billowing the sheers out, ruffling PATRICK's hair and suit jacket and trousers. Simultaneous with the blinding light and the blast of wind, the sound of the church bells louden to an earsplitting pitch. A beat.
Blackout.)

END OF PLAY

FURNITURE, COSTUMES AND PROPS

FURNITURE
Standard bed (on raised platform)
2 night tables (Italian if possible, on raised platform)
Chest of drawers (Italian if possible)
Venetian-style mirror (above chest of drawers)
Luggage rack
Round upholstered dressing ottoman (brocade if possible)
Club chair
Club settee (for 2, both of same brocade if possible)
Small coffee table (Italian if possible)

ROOM DRESSING
Linen sheets and European square pillowcases on "turned-down" bed
Matching brocade headboard and dust ruffle on bed
2 swivel wall lamps (L. and R. of bed over night tables)
Venetian-style sconces with half-shades on walls
Brocade curtains (glass doors to balcony in R. wall)
Sheer center curtains (doors to balcony in R. wall)

PROPS ONSTAGE
Hotel tray with bottle of mineral water and glass on R. bedside table
Telephone and separate panel with floor service buttons on L. bedside table
Toilet articles and zipper case on chest of drawers
Patrick's matching luggage: one or two packed suitcases and briefcase
    on floor; half-packed suitcase on luggage rack
Hotel shallow wicker basket with fresh laundry ("silk" shorts and
    various solid-colored shirts)
Pair of shined Italian loafers (Patrick's) on piece of paper on top of
    laundry basket
Cleaned and pressed light summer suit on hanger over back of club chair
Hotel towels (visible on towel rack in O.S.L. bath)
"Non Distubare" ("Do Not Disturb") sign on center doorknob
European lock on center door (permits 3 revolutions of key)
Matches and ashtray on coffee table

<u>PROPS OFFSTAGE</u>
Hotel tray with
    2 demitasse cups and saucers
    1 espresso pot (for 2) with coffee
    container for sugar packs
    1 liqueur glass
    Genepy bottle (or 1 crystal decanter with green "liqueur")
    room service bill and pen (for Waiter)
Patrick's new soft, black (velour if possible) bedroom slippers (to fit
    Conrad)

<u>COSTUMES AND PROPS ON CHARACTERS</u>
PATRICK
    Creased off-white (cream or beige) linen suit
    Open collar, long sleeve white shirt
    Italian loafers (no socks)
    Pair of dark glasses
    Hotel room key (European style key with metal medallion with
        number or a tassel instead of medallion)
    Various shopping bags from "designer" stores (Armani, Gucci,
        Cartier, etc.) which Patrick enters holding at top of show

CONRAD
    Black suit with white Roman collar and black bib
    Black shoes and socks
    Pair of dark glasses
    Patrick's new black velour slippers (Conrad's size)
    Pack of cigarettes (in pocket)

WAITER
    Black shoes and socks
    Black trousers
    Strong commercial hotel jacket
    White shirt with wing collar and white bow tie
    Black cummerbund
    Hotel insignia pin (brass "H") or Italian flag pin worn on lapel

CORRIDOR BACKING

BACKING

TOWEL RACK

DOOR TO BATH

BATH

LUGGAGE RACK

CHEST OF DRAWERS

TABLE

TABLE

BED

PLATFORM

OTTOMAN

FRONT DOOR TO SUITE

SETTEE

COFFEE TABLE

CLUB CHAIR

DRAPES — SHEER CURTAINS — DRAPES

DOOR

BALCONY RAIL

TRINITA DEI MONTI (CHURCH STEEPLE) ROANOKE BACKING

FOR REASONS THAT REMAIN UNCLEAR